A Summer with the Searchers

By Paul Slevin

D1824186

To my wife Marion and kids Paul and Aimee for their love and support.

Acknowledgement

To family and friends who helped make this book possible by their continued faith and support.

Thanks go to my proof readers

Frank McCulloch, Philip McShane, Linda McAuslan and Mark Cooney.

Special thanks go to

Pamela Smith and Angela Russell for final editing

Kieran Reilly for the front cover design

Andrew Slevin for I.T. input and final publishing

Table of contents

Chapter 1

As local summer's go, this one had offered nothing out of the ordinary so far. The golden sun above, having made her annual pact with the not so sparse cloud cover below, had began playing hide and seek with her glorious rays.

Pale freckled bodies everywhere wisely use the dull spells to top up on various lotions that would transform their colourless bodies into the bronzed, unblemished sort seen on American TV. For most though, simply not turning a blistered pink would be an accomplishment.

One person however, down below and not paying particular attention to God's mediocre handing out of summer to the townsfolk, was Paul Joseph O'Hare. PJ had just completed another year of school, coping with his exams quite comfortably but felt at a crossroads in his life where a good education was essential but the term 'school leaver' appealed even more so, at times. Days had come and gone where he had no idea which direction to go but, more worryingly, recently there were days in which he wasn't exactly sure of the direction he had just come.

At sixteen, he had a rough idea which direction his parents thought was best but if he pondered too much over the issue, it often brought him considerable discomfort. So, for now, all future plans were put on hold. His concentration would be focused on enjoying the holidays whilst combining a part-time job at the local supermarket with the love of his life, football.

Summertime in Scotland usually means packing some skimpy clothes into a suitcase and heading off somewhere guaranteed to come out victorious in the search for sun. Unfortunately, PJ and his family had to miss out on a plane trip to a tan this year due to dad's work commitments. Mr O'Hare, a driving instructor, had too many students waiting on test dates and needed to be available at short notice over the next two months. At least PJ could look forward to free driving lessons next March when he turned seventeen. Last year's three hour delay in Tenerife airport also helped take the edge off of the disappointment of not going abroad. The family plan was to jump into the car at every opportunity and set off in any direction. 'See where the trip takes us,' Mr O'Hare had said. So far they had managed only one trip up north but came home early because of heavy, continuous rain and body battering winds. Little did PJ know, a journey lay ahead that would change all their lives for ever.

Smiling, he absorbed the chants and singing. Noise echoed up to the old metal roof of the north stand, colliding with the next wave, already exploding into a downward path. PJ gazed around at the mayhem inside Coalbridge Rovers FC ground.

After only a few moments of soaking up the electric atmosphere, sound and vision brought him to a frightening realisation. They were chanting his name. 'PJ, PJ!' Before he had a chance to come to terms with this unusual event, he also became aware of yelling from the sidelines. Bob Kennedy, who had only recently won Manager of the Year for leading Coalbridge Rovers to the League Title, stood ranting at him.

'C'mon son, move!'

Why would he be shouting at me? PJ's heart nearly stopped as he felt something underfoot. It was the ball. Only then did he finally notice that he was on the park playing football against his heroes. Mr Kennedy wasn't the only one interested in him. Stuart Gray barged into his back.

'Alright big man,' smiled PJ, rolling the ball around while holding off the giant Coalbridge captain. Gray pulled PJ's shirt, knocking him off balance.

'Carry it!' screamed Mr Kennedy.

Stuff this, why not have a go? It's not every day you get a chance to play football with these guys. Using all his strength, he leaned back into the defender and cutely flicked the ball through his legs. Another touch freed him from the now following Gray.

One of the most important words in the football bible is pace. Unfortunately, some fall victim to the dreaded two words - no pace. Most seasoned professionals, sooner or later get a visit from the grim reaper that arrives in three words, 'legs have gone.' Neither of the latter were going to be a problem to PJ for a long time. Fully trained and finely tuned in the art form of 'let's get the hell out of here quick,' during a decade of boyhood pranks in the back streets and dimly lit lanes of Coalbridge had added endurance to PJ's natural pace. Making himself scarce at speed wasn't only useful and quite essential to healthy living back then but was proving to be a welcome asset at present.

Bob Kennedy stood at the edge of the playing field screeching 'Pass!' in a way that if the letters P and S were removed from his desperate wailing, it would surely sound like a man had just been fired off the top of a very high cliff.

'I can do this!' shouted PJ as a few more strides took him further away from the puffing and panting of the struggling player behind. 'I thought he was faster, maybe his legs have gone,' mumbled PJ, concentrating on the quickly approaching McPherson.

'Pass!' was still being wrenched out of Mr Kennedy, obviously not having completed his journey to the bottom of the mountain. PJ used the old 'double skip over' to breeze past McPherson. He almost allowed himself to think it was too easy when his glorious run came to an abrupt end, courtesy of Tam McAdam, partner in crime to Gray.

PJ entered dreamland momentarily as a giant hand suddenly appeared, unseen to all around, knocking him upwards into a kaleidoscope full of wonderful colour. After shaking him around like a Bloody Mary, he was tipped upside down and emptied onto the ground, colours and all. Numbness accompanied a feeling of dampness from the pitch. A strange but reassuring voice inside his head filled him with a peculiar inviting contentment to lie on the comfortable grass a while longer.

'PASS!' was still echoing somewhere in the far distance. Several annoying blades of grass sticking up PJ's nose brought him slowly to the decision that the giant hand still remained at work.

Convincing himself that the unwelcome intruder would disperse if he could only move,

PJ forced himself over onto his back and began the task of opening eyelids. Into focus came a bright blue sky. The clouds, high above, resembled a cotton wool staircase stretching and reaching out, carving a route upwards into oblivion until it was replaced by a dripping wet sponge impacting on his unguarded face. *I preferred the clouds,* thought PJ as the magic sponge went into overdrive. He blinked and spluttered while trying to breathe during the onslaught. The strange cloud formation disappeared, leaving behind only a white.

'Sorry wee man,' PJ's eyes opened instantly to the smiling face of Tam McAdam, 'I think I hit you a bit hard there.'

'Nah, I've been hit harder by the cold,' lied PJ.

Big Tam laughed momentarily before being knocked out of vision. Red around the gills, saliva fired its way towards PJ like a Spitfire aeroplane showering its target below. 'I said PASS son!' ranted Mr Kennedy. PJ tried to focus on the face while doing his best to avoid the watery assault. 'How hard can it be to kick a ball to another player?' continued the angry manager. PJ lay on the grass, transfixed. Bob Kennedy seemed a bit upset as he handed out his abundance of knowledge. PJ knew that whatever the great man was saying probably would be worth listening to, but found himself wondering, *'if it's sunny then why is this grass so wet?'*

Volume suddenly returned to the fast moving lips of Mr Kennedy. Probably down to the giant hands, intent on totally ruining PJ's day. 'I told you to pass son!' screamed the manager grabbing PJ by the shoulders, shaking him backwards and forwards. PJ closed his eyes hoping everything would go away. *If only I had a towel to dry my face and an interpreter to help me understand what this lunatic is trying to tell me.*

Clear as a summer's day, which can be rare in this part of the world, the manager's voice changed to a more familiar sound but PJ couldn't quite make out who it belonged to.

'Can you hear me?' enquired the voice. PJ lay flat on his back, eyes firmly closed. *Why all the fuss about a late pass? I should have thumped the ball anywhere.*

'PJ get up.'

'Beat it, I'm not playing anymore.'

'Get up now, you're late for work!'

PJ opened his eyes fast and wide to the last request, having worked out that the owner of the familiar voice was his older brother James. He looked every bit as angry and as loud as the Coalbridge manager.

Finally realising he was lying in bed, PJ sprung up into a sitting position. James stared at him for a few seconds before bursting into laughter.

'Let me guess, it was one of your football or Christina dreams wasn't it?'

PJ didn't answer, too busy trying to recall his latest sleeping adventure.

'You were shouting, 'I can do this!' when I came into the room,' said James, stooping over his wee brothers startled face. Again PJ didn't reply.

'Well did you?'

'Did I what?' said PJ eventually.

'Do whatever you said you could do,' laughed James. PJ decided to end the brief conversation, turning away from his brother's smug glare. James took the hint and moved off. PJ tried to recall the weird dream. James dropped some training gear untidily onto the bed, fumbled through various tops and shorts, then threw the chosen garments into his open bag. He pulled the strings, binding it closed. PJ stared straight ahead as if in a deep trance, He still couldn't make any sense out of this latest episode of abnormal sleeping activity, Coalbridge Rovers, Bob Kennedy and co, or getting hacked from behind by Tam McAdam.

James yanked his training bag off of the computer chair causing it to spin and creating a whirring sound that only added to PJ's confusion. *I can't believe big Tam fouled me like that.* The spinning chair came to a halt bringing back silence and reality slowly to the half wakened boy. James playfully grabbed him by the chin, 'See ya!'

PJ pushed the annoying hand away. Any thought of falling back to sleep was removed as James banged the bedroom door shut behind him. 'Get up!' he shouted, thumping downstairs. PJ knew that James would report back to mum at the first opportunity. Trouble definitely loomed not far away. To be honest, he did have a lot more dreams about football than those occasional Christina Aguilera ones but statistics weren't going to matter after Tuesday Night

PJ had fallen into a contented sleep on the couch while watching highlights from the English Premier league. Mum carried out a deep discussion, probably about nothing in particular, via a telephone call with Aunt Jean. All of a sudden, PJ started chanting rude words at a man dressed in black. It was lucky mum had a scatter cushion at her disposal. She launched it across the room, catching him on the head. Fortunately, he wakened before blurting out the nasty part about the man and his family status. After a look at the cushion lying next to him along with harsh stares from mum, PJ knew he had been at it again. Avoiding eye contact, he sat the cushion carefully back on the couch, patted it then headed to bed, hopeful that Aunt Jean could keep mum captivated in conversation long enough for him to get to sleep, more dreams. *What next?* P.J thought , sinking down into his pillow.

Jack Watson gazed over gleaming aisles. Fully stacked shelves made a welcome sight. From a raised office in 'Watson and Son,' he stood, arms folded, casting an experienced eye to every detail of his small empire. The office had never really changed much through the years other than the necessary addition of computer ware. Screensaver monitors kept a watchful eye on piles of paperwork scattered across busy looking desks. Long before computers were a must to any business, Jack happened to stroll into Bells Groceries looking for a job.

Sam Bell, who owned the store, had noticed an honest face in the friendly young character.

'Start on Monday son, see how you get on.'

As it turned out, Sam got it right. Jack tended to every task asked of him, eventually becoming manager of Bells Groceries. Years of hard graft, plus a fair price from the old man meant that Jack could buy the store. Friendship and a small dose of luck allowed further expansion. Bells Groceries became Watson and Son. One day Jack would put his feet up, relax at home or spend endless hours on the Golf Course while son Joseph took care of the family business. Jack's roving eyes swept over confectionary into soft drinks where young Joe stood, piling bottles of coke onto a special offer display. Clumsy wires dangled out of his pocket from the MP4 player that dad had told him not to bring to work on several occasions. The music pumping into his ears caused head nodding movements like he was saying yes to an imaginary friend. Jack knew that golf and relaxing would need to wait a while.

Years of experience had taught Jack all the tricks of the trade. Old Sam's motto was, 'Bring 'em in and make 'em buy.' Jack simply added availability and variety as his own. Give people a great choice at a good price. So far it had worked.

Finishing his daily inspection, not only did Jack notice Mrs Chambers running ten minutes late as she headed for her milk, or that the glistening sheen was steadily being buffed and scuffed from the foyer floor by the early rush of Saturday shoppers. Something else didn't seem to be quite in place. It took no more than a minute for him to work out the problem. PJ was late again.

Meanwhile, back at home, PJ practised the 'sorry I'm late' speech while straightening his tie in the hall mirror. Half sleeping blue eyes tried hard to focus while he prodded gelled blonde locks into a messy look. Five minutes later, after a quick trip through the kitchen he finally set off for work. Munching on a half slice of toast, he went through part of the excuse where mum forgot to set the alarm. That one should do the trick.

Bodies skilfully missed each other coming in and going from Watson and Son's front door. PJ smiled and greeted those who made eye contact with him. That supermarket bland buzz met his arrival on the shop floor. Before he could adjust to the shop environment, PJ got distracted by Joe who was signalling with both arms towards the warehouse. This being the signal that his dad was there and PJ should go in the other direction. Joe then turned away as if he hadn't just resembled an Aircraft Controller on a Flight Deck. Joe seemed to be able to do such things with very little effort. He turned back momentarily to receive PJ's verification on avoiding Dad. When he did so, his leg bumped into Mrs Simpson's trolley, which then thumped into the stationery trolley of Mr Robertson while he decided on white or yellow rice. Unfortunately, before he could get the chance to drop the Chinese style yellow rice into his trolley, it was gone, in the direction of old Jimmy Henderson. Poor Jimmy was leaning forward admiring the crust on his steak pie when the metal intruder knocked him down.

Luckily, Jimmy's fall was cushioned slightly by the 'pie for four' leaving the imprint of his chin moulded within the guaranteed 80% meat interior.

PJ decided to head for his second hideout, a small storeroom behind the fresh fish counter. Joe followed close behind, unaware that Mr Henderson now lay among a pile of chocolate chip cookies, gazing at the new shape of his pie. Jack arrived at the scene immediately to put things right. He promptly exchanged Jimmy's chin ridden pie for another while paying particular attention to not laughing. Jack apologised and assured Mr Henderson he wouldn't need to buy either pie.

'Are you ok Jimmy, let me take your messages over to the check outs. I think you've earned them for nothing today,' smiled Jack.

'That's awful nice of you son, I'm as well taking the damaged pie too,' replied Jimmy with a wink.

'No problem.' *You fly old goat,* thought Jack keeping his smile in check. Although Joe was nowhere to be seen, he would have bet another ten steak pies that his son would have something to do with that fracas.

PJ waited until Joe had removed his ear phones before speaking.

'Alright mate?'

'Afternoon.'

'Funny guy, what's your dad saying?'

Joe picked up a large, frozen, silvery coloured fish, shaking the ice particles down in a spray that covered the other unlucky inhabitants below. He gave PJ a replay of Jack's last words regarding his lateness while the fish carried out mouth movements.

'That lad better have a good excuse this time.'

Noticing how suddenly PJ stopped laughing, Joe dropped the fish into the box and turned to face the boss.

'Hi dad, I was just showing PJ our wide variety of frozen fish.'

'Office, both of you!'

Much later, after a lot of guidance on responsibilities and timekeeping, the boys shrugged off their newly taken on board advice to concentrate on more important matters. They had a 3pm kick off against Thornton Boys Club. Jack watched on as they disappeared through the sliding doors into warm sunshine, wishing he could go to the game with them. He hadn't managed getting to a match for a few weeks now. It was always a great game when these two teams played against each other. Seeing the smug gloating smile being wiped off Thornton manager Bert Wallace's face if his team got beaten was enough incentive for anyone to attend a football match. Maybe Jack would make an effort today.

Chapter 2

Sunshine, being rudely interrupted by wandering cloud, came as a welcome relief to the gradually tiring body of Frankie Milne, mid-thirties, plumber, DIY enthusiast and self-confessed believer in 'your body is a temple'. On the road for nearly an hour, his temple roof was beginning to thin a little and foundations showing ageing cracks plus worrying signs of wall enlargement. Never the less, five more minutes would take him into Witchwood Forest. From there, another nineteen at seven minute mile pace through the valley, back out into Melrose Place to a time of 1hr-28mins.

Frankie had finished this particular route only once before, inside 1hr-30. As he slowly picked up pace, his limbs, confused by the decision, immediately went into talks and agreed on a build up of lactic acid to convince Frankie that stopping would be a good idea. If this didn't do the trick then a stitch in the side was next. Totally focused and oblivious to the stirring pain whirling up from the unanimous decision by internal body affairs to stop, Frankie trundled down Sloan Terrace onto the dirt footpath that wound its way into the forest.

Witchwood Forest holds a certain beauty that only summer can begin to captivate. Each season brings it's very own brand of genius carved by God's hand. Summer though, was enchanting, set apart from the rest. Unimaginable arrangements of wild flowers nestled in an array of deep green. Birds harmonised various tunes as here and there daily chores were carried out. Tall trees proudly reached up, branches outstretched while feeding on the Sun's warmth.

Colour and shadow danced freely below, accompanied by a whispering breeze, gently cooling everything in her path.

She certainly couldn't have missed the fast approaching PJ weaving his way through the narrow footpaths that swung down onto the tar mac lane, leading to Thornton. Every touch on his brake lever caused the back wheel to kick up bark chips, spraying them, confetti at a wedding style, over nature's wonders. Nature would need to wait on PJ's acceptance of her beauty. He had a game to get to. More important in his mind was the chat with mum earlier that ultimately resulted in him missing the team minibus to Thornton. Thanks to big brother James who bumped into mum at the sports centre, Mrs O'Hare had hurried home to discuss the latest episode of 'PJ at Night'. He had heard the key turn, clicking the front door open and made a break for it out the back door but mum caught him half way up the driveway.

PJ was then persuaded back inside to talk about things like unbroken sleep without the need for chanting, among some other issues.

By the time mum had finished the ear bashing, PJ knew the minibus would have already departed. He promised to stop shouting out stuff when sleeping then quickly got his bike from the shed. Moments later PJ was pedalling out of Springfield Place, eyes fixed firmly ahead while contemplating the quickest route to Thornton.

He opted for a shortcut through Witchwood Forest. It would bring him out right at the playing fields.

Not only did PJ have the odd restless night, he was also guilty of concentrating on the wrong thing at the wrong time. This feature in itself isn't such a bad thing but is not to be advised when travelling at speed on a bike.

That goalie is poor with cross balls. I can get past their left back no problem and whip some balls into the box.

PJ hurtled down through the narrow path, brushing bush and branches aside, mind totally focused on the Thornton goalie. This caused him to forget a more pressing issue which was contributing to his arrival on the main drag sooner than he expected. Speed.

I'll fire loads of crosses over to big Stevie. 'Arghh!'

His back wheel locked as he skidded across the lane, coming to a halt fractionally before the smooth surface became thick grass. All to the sheer delight of Mrs Muir who had just finished collecting her little dog Zack's business into a bag via her poop scoop. She forgot the task momentarily as PJ trundled towards her. Zack stared at the contents of the bag, now clinched into a fist, while his Mistress and the cyclist regained their senses.

'Sorry,' said PJ eventually. He tried not to look at the still moving mess in the old ladies hand.

'It's alright son, no harm done,' replied Mrs Muir. She was becoming aware though, of her warm grip. The rebellious contents were threatening to leave her hand. PJ gave a courteous nod of the head before setting off. Pedalling away; he noticed an approaching jogger. Oh no, that's Moaner Milne, he knows Dad.

Now within shouting distance, Mr Milne began waving his arms while showering PJ with menacing words about road safety. PJ answered the tirade of abuse by simply raising a hand. This wasn't to admit the fault but to advise that all communication should be directed to it. Pleased by the reaction, PJ dismissed the jogger and continued on his way.

He had only redirected his concentration to ways of passing defender Martin Steele when a most peculiar sensation washed over him. Everything stopped, like pause on a DVD player. A yellow mist suddenly appeared on the ground around him. It swirled into golden ribbons, engulfing him as it rose. The world fell silent and still, then, BANG!

PJ felt a slight numbness before realising that he stood, staring once again at Mrs Muir. The old lady seemed unaware of any previous meeting. Golden sparks fizzled away but the mist remained in his head. Unsure of what to say this time, PJ apologised and set off towards the oncoming runner. Mr Milne didn't look as cocky this time. Reaching each other, they both stopped. PJ shook his head trying to remove the golden haze that was blurring his vision. Frankie Milne looked edgy. He pressed a button on his stopwatch then double checked it.

PJ smiled. I must be having one of these weird realistic dreams. He recalled the one when he scored the winning goal for Scotland, celebrating with his team mates. Mum pulled the pillow off him as he rolled around the bedroom floor. This feels a bit different but at least I'm beginning to control them. I may as well enjoy myself.

'Still rubbish at golf Frankie boy?'

Mr Milne didn't answer. Instead he tapped his wristwatch.

'Is it true that raindrops gently roll down a window pane quicker than you approach a finish line?'

PJ laughed at Mr Milne's reluctance to defend his athletic ability.

'I think there's something wrong with my watch son!'

'If your watch is running at all then it's doing better than you!'

Mission accomplished, PJ pedalled away content that he'd got the better of moaner Milne for the first time in his life.

Heading for Thornton felt like the thing to do so off he went.

'Oh no!'

The golden swirl once again weaved and curled around the spokes of his bike, rising menacingly until he was enveloped. He braced himself. BANG!

PJ stared at the forgiving face of Mrs Muir for the third time. Little Zack though, had a doggy style expression of 'something weird is happening'. Mrs Muir assured PJ once again that no harm had been done. He replied with the now customary 'sorry' then pedalled off again.

I think I've had just about enough of this dream.

Mr Milne stopped as PJ approached. Both stared at each other. PJ wasn't quite sure what to say so stated simply,

'Alright !'

Frankie Milne took a step forward, eyes narrowing.

'Raindrops rolling down a window pane...' he muttered.

'That's nice, is it a poem?'

'No, it's what you said to me last time!'

PJ felt a bit sorry for Mr Milne so decided to put him out of his misery.

'Look Frankie boy, don't panic. You're caught up in one of my mad dreams. Somebody usually wakens me up about now.'

'Listen son! Forget poems and window panes. It's true, there are better golfers and athletes than myself but I have a slight problem with your dream!'

Mr Milne's panting ceased as he continued.

'Can I add something to your dream? Frankie boy's not sleeping!'

Unable to speak, PJ let the new information sink in while giving his lips a chance to work. It seemed like an eternity of silence. Mr Milne awaited an answer. One which PJ couldn't possibly give. His fuzzy head offered only three options. Laugh, cry or run.

A sharp outburst of laughter shattered the silence. PJ broke away from the staring match to investigate.

The sound came from a thick cluster of bush high up on the grass embankment. PJ concentrated on the area, unaware that his bike had just fallen to the ground. Before actually realising what was happening, he found himself half way up the steep bank, eyes fixed on thick greenery directly below a giant Oak tree. Twigs snapping underfoot alerted him that he was close enough.

'Who's there?' asked PJ in a feeble voice.

As expected, the bush didn't answer.

He cleared his throat then proceeded with silly statement number two.

'I know you're there!'

This time the bush shuddered uncontrollably for a few moments, trailing off into an eerie silent stillness that left PJ feeling alone and scared.

He looked back down the slope hoping for some backup from Mr Milne, only to find the runner leaning forward over the fallen bike. Frankie stood as if still in conversation.

Along the lane Mrs Muir's statue like figure kept a firm grip of the unpleasant contents belonging to little Zack.

PJ was most certainly alone. He took a slow step backwards, unfortunately catching his heel on a protruding tree root, menacingly sticking up through the wild grass. Off he went on a quick downward journey, collecting various twigs and leaves on the way. He finally stopped rolling on a flat verge at the lane's edge, jumping to his feet instantly.

'Somebody please waken me up!' shouted PJ, arms outstretched.

His pleading voice filtered away into another uncomfortable silence. It was time for plan B. Get on the bike and go.

Alarm bells were ringing in his head. PJ was starting to realise this might not be a dream. Picking up the bike, he waved a hand in front of Mr Milne's face, gaining no reaction from the frozen man.

PJ wanted to pedal away but felt responsible for Mr Milne and Mrs Muir. His vision became obscured again as he tried focusing on the area below the big Oak tree. He let the bike drop again and took a few cautious steps up the slope.

'Who are you?' he yelled, blinking while trying to keep eye contact through the golden fuzz.

'You must leave now,' said a voice from within the bushes.

It caused PJ to take a few steps back, before asking, 'Is this a dream?'

'Of sorts,' replied the strange unfamiliar voice.

'I've never spoken to a bush in one of my dreams.'

PJ's comment sent the bushes into a shaking convulsion that he couldn't see due to his head being full of thick, swirling cloud.

'You must go,' insisted the voice once again.

PJ felt so confused by this point that further questions were not required. He picked up his recently dropped bike and got on.

Mr Milne and Mrs Muir remained in their trance as he began pedalling away. Without looking back, he asked one last question.

'Will I remember this dream?'

'Perhaps,' answered a friendlier voice.

Before PJ could pick up pace, someone pressed the pause button on his world.

He froze, watching the curling, golden shimmer dance around him.

'Oh no!'

BANG!

PJ pedalled away from Mrs Muir unaware at this precise moment of having done so on three previous occasions.

On passing Mr Milne, both exchanged only pleasant smiles this time. Mr Milne appeared to be more interested in his wristwatch than saying hello. He tapped it frantically as PJ sped past.

Once out of the forest PJ swerved into Thorntonhill Rd. His head had cleared of the earlier fuzz but he felt strange. It took a few more seconds before realising where he was supposed to be going. Like emerging out of a teenage daydream, PJ simply dismissed his momentary lack of memory and redirected his thoughts to ways of getting balls into the Thornton box.

At the back of his mind though, he couldn't quite rid himself of the word, 'perhaps'.

An annoying feeling of forgetting to do something plagued him as he pedalled down towards the football parks.

At the same time, Frankie Milne managed to quell the rebellion in his inner temple, urged on by this unbelievably fast pace. The build up of lactic acid had joined forces with Frankie's positive thought. Between them, they conquered the painfully increasing stitch in his side. Adrenalin did the rest.

Frankie would soon be out of the forest into Melrose Place. He took another peek at his watch just to be sure. Indeed, a personal best time of 1hr-30 was about to be cut by 32 minutes.

Frankie exited Witchwood Forest like champion Sebastian Coe crossing an Olympic finish line, regardless of a possible faulty watch, or a possible heart attack.

Meanwhile, Mrs Muir dropped the bag of dog poo into a waste bin and continued her walk with Zack.

There was no fooling the little dog though. He knew something weird had just taken place.

Chapter 3

Big Tam McGonnagle stood outside the changing rooms, too angry to venture inside just at the moment. He took a drag on his Benson and Hedges fag, eyes fixed on the blue sky above while trundling through a bunch of what ifs. Grey smoke clouded his vision every now and again. The Bridge East manager couldn't find much fault in his team's performance. A lack of concentration cost us a silly goal, thought Tam, unconsciously flicking his finished fag in the direction of a Fiat Punto owned by Thornton manager Bert Wallace. Well, almost unconsciously. Bert was a bit of a prat who liked to rub salt into the wounds of losing teams, especially Bridge East. I better get in and speak to the boys, decided Tam.

He swung the changing room door open with renewed vigour.

"C'mon boys, heads up, we'll get them next time. What did I say about that goalie being poor with cross balls?"

PJ's eyes began to water as he raced down Thornton hill Rd. From here you could view most of Thornton and in particular, the playing fields that were the home ground of Thornton boys club. At least the quick flowing breeze cleared his head of, we'll see, allowing him to enjoy the waited anticipation.

He pedalled through the car park, slowly filling up with adrenalin.

Joe sat, half listening to Tam's usual after match team talk, wondering how PJ managed to miss the game. Throwing his worn top onto the bundle already there in the centre of the busy changing room, he headed for a shower hoping the warm water could remove all memory of Thornton's victory along with the sticky sweat.

'Sorry I'm late guys' said PJ casually, after bursting into the room. Silence ate into Tam's we'll get them next time speech. Everyone watched on as PJ began empting his bag, continuing with his verbal downfall of the opposition. 'I'm going to wander out wide so get plenty of balls over to me, that goalie is dodgy'

Kicking his boots under the bench, PJ didn't bother turning around so, was unaware of the staring faces and the pile of dirty football strips lying in a pile on the floor. He began undressing. Joe overheard the commotion just before stepping into the shower, as did the others in the shower room. All eyes were now on PJ.

After a brief pause, Tam managed to regain control of his mouth. 'Where have you been son?' he asked.

PJ was either so excited about the game or obviously still suffering some after effects from the golden fuzz. He didn't even notice wee Sid

Savage sitting, slumped next to him. Sid who played left wing back could run all day but gave the impression of having central heating installed in his cheeks after five minutes of every game. PJ laughed while telling his story about getting caught and lectured by Mum. 'So you missed the minibus then' said Tam in a quiet concerned voice.

'Yeh, I had to come on my bike' answered PJ, finally turning around. Noticing the stunned faces, he added 'look guys I'm sorry I missed the minibus but are we not making a big deal about nothing here'

A grunt of muffled laughter somewhere at the back of the room triggered another. Tam quickly silenced the chuckles with a loud "shut it everybody" He looked back at PJ and cleared his throat.

'You didn't just miss the minibus son; you've missed the entire game. We got beaten one nil in case you're interested!' Tam's comment caused the stunned faces around to soften with the twangs of amusement. Joe barged through to the front of PJ's audience.

'Are you alright mate?' The room now became peppered with sporadic sniggering that added to the rising tension. Tam shouted for silence again but the sudden hush was worse than the laughter.

PJ wanted the ground to open up and give him the opportunity to fall down into nothingness. Anything would be better than this lot right now.

Within seconds, he had dressed and repacked his bag.

'Look, I tried my best to make the game' stated a feeble embarrassed PJ already heading for the door. A voice from the crowd answered, 'Not bad mate, only two hours late.' This comment fuelled the inevitable. PJ quickly departed the changing room amidst roars of laughter. Any doubts about missing the game were finally removed by the smug face of Bert Wallace in the corridor.

'Better luck next time wee man' smiled Bert. 'What happened to you today anyway?' he added.

PJ was so confused that he almost forgot to insult the Thornton manager. Brushing past him into he late afternoon sunshine, he turned to see Bert still watching, as if waiting on a reply. 'Good result Mr Wallace, are you putting on weight or is it just the track suit'

'Cheeky wee git' answered Bert. He waited until PJ had disappeared across the car park before taking a reassuring peek at his new trackie.

Joe decided to give the shower a miss. He was out of the changing room in minutes after PJ. Big Bert seemed to be checking himself out in the reception window as Joe passed by. 'Too bad son' muttered the victorious manager.

Joe kept walking without looking back. 'Nice tracksuit Bert, did ye get a hippo to break it in for you'

'Cheeky wee git' shouted Bert, trying to smooth down the wrinkled nylon.

Joe let his eyes adjust to the bright sunshine then wandered off in the direction of the last remaining game being played. Bridge East under fourteens were finishing a late kick off against their Thornton counter parts. Joe dropped his bag and slumped down next to PJ.

'That wee number seven's a good player'

PJ nodded in agreement. Joe took in a few moments of the game, not wanting to make matters worse but couldn't help himself.

'What's happening mate, are you going nuts?'

'Must be' replied PJ'.

Both boys sat in silence following the game half heartedly while cradling their individual worries. PJ tried going through his day again and again but found it more confusing each time. Joe on the other hand bounced only one prominent thought and conclusion around his worried mind. My mate has lost the plot.

A three each draw unfolded before them. By the time the ref blew the final whistle. Joe was bursting with questions. For now, he would avoid the obvious ones like, when is the clinic taking you in for observation.

'You never miss a game PJ'

This question was designed to stir PJ towards gradually opening up. Joe hoped they could at least agree on something before falling out. A number of answers would have been sufficient. I know or I don't know what happened, could have eased the situation. Joe wasn't prepared for the eventual answer.

'I didn't

'You didn't what?'

Joe stood up, looking really uncomfortable. 'Can we clear up the little mistake you just made there?'

'What mistake?'

'The one where you said you didn't miss the game'

'Something happened to me'

'Wow, PJ has left the building'

'You've got to believe me'

'Lift off', laughed.

PJ jumped to his feet. 'I'm telling the truth'

'Coalbridge we have a problem'

'Look,' answered PJ holding up his arm to let Joe see

The watch, 'It's at 3:15.' Joe took a quick peek but wasn't to be persuaded.

'You've totally gone PJ. Let me know if there is life on Pluto while you're up there.'

PJ turned away from Joe, feeling the need to bitch slap him, too strong. Tempers simmered slightly in the following silence. PJ attempted once more to get Joe on his side. 'My watch is never wrong' Joe picked up his bag, and turned to PJ.

'It probably stopped due to the temperature on re-entry to Earth!'

Another uneasy silence crept in. PJ turned away again, this time staring up towards Witchwood Forest.

He could remember everything from this morning until going in there. Mrs Muir, Mr Milne and little Zack all meant something to him. We'll see, we'll see.

PJ walked away from Joe without saying another word.

'Where are you going now?' asked a baffled Joe.

'I'm going to nip up to Pluto; I'll let you know if I find any life!'

'I'm being serious here mate, what am I supposed to think. You disappeared for two hours today'

'No I didn't'

'Wow, now you're scaring me' replied Joe.

Joe felt a little hard done by and pretty much unappreciated. He had already waved off the team coach, wishing now that he hadn't. PJ strolled off in the direction of the pavilion to get his bike. Against his better judgement Joe followed, standing outside until PJ exited pushing the bike. PJ noticed that his friend had not deserted him, yet. This lifted his spirit a bit.

'Do you want backy home?' he asked.

'Might as well' replied Joe, climbing onto the bike. PJ steadied the frame while he got on the seat.

'We'll do a quick stop off in the Forest on the way' said PJ.

'What for?'

'That's where something happened'

'What happened?'

'I Dunno' answered PJ.

Here we go again thought Joe as they set off for Witchwood Forest.

Deep in the Forest, shade was ever increasing as the lowering sun edged west. Branches whispered overhead, nodding to and fro in the early evening breeze.

'Not much further mate' exclaimed PJ, breathing heavily from the journey.

Five minutes later, PJ pulled the brakes. He stepped over the bike frame leaving Joe to steady it. PJ scanned the area like a crime scene.

'I remember coming down that path onto the lane' said PJ, pointing to the shortcut from Coalbridge. Joe let the bike slide to the ground. 'That's the way we would come'

'I know, but this is where things got muddled' decided PJ.

'What do you mean?'

'I came down the path thinking about the game then everything went a bit weird'

'Like it's getting now' remarked Joe. PJ didn't hear the comment. He wandered around, mind going into overdrive trying to connect the path with thoughts in his mind. A tall tree stood amidst thick bushes half way up the grass slope, right where PJ had stopped his bike.

Looking back in the direction of the narrow shortcut, he returned focus to the tree. Starting at the top, branches wavered slowly as his eyes began their journey down the thick trunk until it sank behind dense bushes. After a few moments, he stared back along the lane.

'Mrs Muir was standing over there with her wee dog' stated PJ eventually. He looked the other way and pointed, 'Moaner Milne was jogging here'

'Ok, but what was Mrs Muir doing standing in a forest?'

'She was waving to Mrs Milne.' It must have been some wave, lasting two hours, thought Joe. He didn't bother sharing his assumption with PJ who probably wouldn't have heard anyway. Bits and pieces of recollection were beginning to creep back into his exhausted brain.

'Mrs Muir held something in her hand' muttered PJ Joe watched on as his mate strolled around, ruffling through overworked memory banks.

'Crap' said PJ excitedly.

'Have you forgotten again?'

'No, she held a bag of crap belonging to her wee dog'

'Why would somebody in the middle of a Forest bother putting crap in a bag?'

Both boys looked at each other and agreed, 'Dunno'

'Right, now were getting somewhere, how does Moaner Milne fit into you're day?' asked Joe.

'I think I might have insulted him'

'Brilliant, what did you say?'

'Dunno' admitted PJ. Joe seemed a little disappointed. 'Are you not hungry mate?'

'I'm starving'

'Good, why don't you stop staring at that tree and let's go home for dinner. We'll talk about your nervous breakdown at the club tonight'

'I spoke to someone up there' said PJ, pointing up the steep slope.

'PJ it's a tree, please don't tell me you were talking to a tree'

'No it was that bush in front of the tree'

'Wow, too far, I'm out of here.'

'Joe please! I need you to trust me'

Joe looked up at the totally normal woodland scenery.

Concern was growing not only for PJ's sanity but his own. He grabbed PJ by the arm, dragging him up the slope. They made their way around the conspicuous bush like Shaggy and Scooby, stopping at a small flattened area in the wiry grass.

'Told you!', stated PJ triumphantly. Joe could only agree. Somebody definitely had knelt or sat there recently. 'You're right, let's go eat some food now', replied Joe, already half way back down the slope. PJ followed close behind, trying to recall anything of importance. It was no use. Recollection brought only more confusion. They got on the bike and headed home. PJ arrived at the corner of Joe's street, after twenty minutes of blabbing on about talking bushes and golden fuzz, among other things. His mate had stopped listening ten minutes ago.

'I'm going to find out what's happening ate, don't worry' said PJ, attempting to play the situation down in proportion.

'No probs get dinner and maybe a wee rest before the Club tonight' Joe disguised his worry using a touch of sarcasm. He watched on as PJ pedalled off, talking to himself.

Joe turned away, hands in pockets. He strolled along Willowbrae Gardens whistling the tune, 'There may be trouble ahead.'

Chapter 4

PJ put his bike into the shed. From where he stood in the back garden, mum could be seen busily moving around the kitchen. Below the window sat a rusty garden bench. Green dust and flakes of paint lay around it. Dad had been promising to restore the old thing for ages and obviously must have made a start. It looked far from being ready for a fresh coat of paint though. Not feeling up to normal family hustle and bustle at the moment, PJ made his way to the summer house at the bottom of the garden. He needed some space and time for a bit of relaxing thought.

This construction was dad's pride and joy. PJ smiled, remembering how much trouble it had been to build. The instructions led dad and James to believe, assemble four easy sides then stick on the roof, In actual fact the information was correct, but when you add a level foundation as a requirement along with the sides needing to be straight, things became a little more difficult. During the erection of the family luxury, tempers frayed. At one point dad and James got into such a bad argument that James threw away the spirit level and threatened to leave home. Dad told him to go but not before paying for a new spirit level. PJ had to intervene and also got carried away, resulting in dad holding a hammer above his head telling him he wouldn't see the light of day for a year. It was only when they realised how pathetic dad looked while wielding the hammer above his head that the whole thing diffused into hilarity.

After a long hard day, father and sons stood back admiring their handy work. Mum hung curtains over the large glass panels. A bamboo framed fabric suite and a bit of furniture finished off the work of art.

PJ left the door open slightly and sunk down onto a floral patterned single sofa. A fresh breeze accepted its invitation from the open door and proceeded to clear the stuffiness inside. Staring at the aimlessly, PJ could remember bits and pieces only. He closed his eyes and began tracing through the day. It was hard to differentiate between what had, had not or maybe happened. Anger escalated as memory diminished. His breathing changed. Unrest welled up from deep within causing an unwanted desire to swallow. Tears filled his eyes.

PJ refused to accept that he was in the early stages of crying. Self-control regained, he wiped the salty wetness from his cheeks and pushed forward on the chair. Both hands became fists. Right, James woke me up this morning, big Macadam hacked me, no he couldn't have, I was dreaming. Mr Watson gave me a row for being late into work, true. Thornton beat us, did they? I wasn't even there. That goalie is rubbish with cross balls, rubbish? Mrs Muir had dog poo in her hand.

'BOO!'

PJ stiffened up before edging off the chair, landing in a heap on the floor.

'Got you!' said his wee sister Annie. Her friendly little face stuck through the open doorway. She had indeed. He didn't even bother looking in the direction of hysterical laughter while picking himself up.

'Yep, I'll give you that one but it's only a matter of time before I get you back,' said PJ rubbing his sore behind. Annie pretended not to hear PJ's idle scaremongering, instead finding something mysteriously interesting in her fingertips. When he had finished, she replied, quite coolly, 'I'll tell dad.'

'Beat it!' yelled PJ.

Annie pulled the door shut and fled. It squeaked as she did so. PJ got back to work. Mr Milne, what did I say to him? Squeak.

Annie popped her head in. 'Are you alright PJ?'

'Yeh small stuff, I just need a minute to think.'

'Oh!'

'Why?'

'Because I told mum you were crying.'

'Brat!' shouted PJ as Annie slammed the door closed in victory. He didn't even get the chance to stand before mum arrived. Squeak. 'I thought your dad was going to oil this door,' she said on entering. 'It's annoying,' agreed PJ as mum sat opposite. 'Dad made it to the second half of the game today.' Mum stood up, moved around in a meaningful manner then sat back down. 'I thought he was working,' said PJ.

'He had a cancellation.' Mum sat forward while she continued, 'He spoke to Jack Watson.'

PJ needed to think quickly. Mum wasn't messing about 'Why didn't you go to the football?' PJ didn't normally make a habit of lying to mum but this was definitely one situation where a little white lie would do no harm. 'I didn't stay.' He felt the urge to jump to his feet, explain exactly just how bizarre the day had been. Then after a reassuring cuddle, be told everything will turn out fine. If only.

In reality, mum, and Annie who was almost most certainly standing outside ear wigging would no doubt run kicking and screaming towards the safety of the house. PJ opted not to share. I was on the way to the game, bumped into a lady holding dog's dirt then disappeared for about two hours.

Mum sat tense, like a quiz show contestant waiting on a final question that could win her the car or world cruise. PJ continued. 'I got there late and Tam dropped me.'

'Why didn't you stay and watch?' enquired mum. This gave PJ and opportunity to capitalise on mum's inexperience of the temperaments involved in football.

'I got angry about being left out so I went for a spin on my bike.' He actually made the load of mince sound quite believable. Mum retreated to a comfy position in her sofa. 'Car and holiday out of reach' 'Is anything bothering you son? Are you worried about your exam results coming next month? It's not the end of the world if you fail them.'

'Mum, you're always telling me to think responsibly and start dealing with life as an adult.' She tried to answer but PJ carried on. 'I've just got a few things that I need to deal with, please, give me some space.'

Mum gave off a loving respectful nod of the head to her boy who implored privacy whilst treading the path to unavoidable adulthood. Inside though, she admitted defeat. Getting up, she smiled and declared, 'There's stovies in the pot.'

'Thanks mum, don't worry.' PJ followed behind whilst mum bundled Annie up into the house.

Dad sat in the lounge browsing through a magazine. PJ wandered past unnoticed. Taking a seat at the dining room table, he waited almost patiently as mum placed a bowl of steaming hot stovies in front of him. She returned a minute later with two slices of plain bread and a mug of steaming hot tea. PJ took a quick look over his feast before getting stuck in. Stovies could help fix any problem.

Ten minutes later, any evidence of a dinner actually having been there were a few breadcrumbs scattered around PJ's cleaned off plate.

Dad threw down the driving instructor's monthly edition and casually strolled into the dining room. 'Bad luck today pal.'

'Sure was,' agreed PJ. Dad walked around the table, eyes lowered as if he'd lost something. Tension stirred up. Even the breadcrumbs on PJ's plate seemed to be waiting on dad's next statement, knowing that a sufficient answer would be required. 'I spoke to Jack Watson today. He told me you were late for work again.' Mum had now returned, locked in eye contact with dad before both parents plus the breadcrumbs turned full attention back to PJ. 'Yeh, I slept in.'

Mum spared PJ any more need for white lies by saying, 'Dad is just a bit worried about you son,' while clearing away the dishes and crumbs. She left PJ staring at the vacant space, still not able to find a solution to the rising interest. Mum filled the dishwasher, pressed a few buttons and flicked the door shut. By the time she stood, arms folded, back in the dining room, dad had edged closer to his son. 'Is anybody bothering you PJ?'

Again she saved PJ's blushes, 'Ahem.'

Dad turned to her. His face carried a look of bewilderment. Cheekbones rose up as if trying to reach the lines in his forehead, which were effortlessly on a downward journey on a collision course with inflated nostrils, PJ wasn't fully versed in the operatic epic, otherwise known as adulthood. He knew though, that dad's intense facial muscle bending was due to confusion. Mum had obviously instructed him earlier, to have a man-to-man chat with his son but since talking to PJ in the summerhouse, she had now decided against it.

'Me and PJ had a wee gab when he came in,' she said.

'Nobody is bothering me dad, honest.'

Dad straightened up, allowed his face a chance at returning to normal. 'Fine.' He wandered back into the lounge, sunk down on his chair and pretended to find something interesting in the driver's magazine. Mum returned to the kitchen and continued her task of moving things around, making a mum-in-the-kitchen sound. Dad looked up from his twice read magazine, 'Alan and Jean are picking us up at eight.' His statement was directed to the kitchen noise. Mum instantly stopped everything. 'I'll never be ready on time!' she exclaimed, rushing through the lounge. Dad and PJ smiled at each other. Normal service had been resumed.

'I see you made a start on the old bench today,' commented PJ from the lounge door.

'It should be finished for next summer,' joked Mr O'Hare.

Before heading upstairs, PJ stopped at the hall mirror. It seemed a lifetime away from when he stood here fixing his tie. Was it only this morning? On arrival at the top stair, his closed bedroom door muffled loud music meaning James had begun the ritual of getting ready for Brannigans. On entering the room James acknowledged his brother with the usual annoying rub of the head.

'Tough luck today,' he said, pulling the wardrobe door open. James gazed into the wardrobe as if his life depended on what clothes he removed from it.

PJ flattened his hair down and sat at the computer. He clicked through various pages until finding his electronic destination, time travel. This had attracted the attention of James whose face suddenly appeared mirror style on the screen. PJ spun around as if guarding a national secret. 'What?'

James smiled, holding a shirt in each hand. 'Which one! white with the pattern or striped with the pattern?'

PJ laughed. 'You've got a crazy dress sense.' 'Cheers,' replied James.

'It wasn't a compliment.'

'That comment would hurt if it came from a guy with class!' James decided himself. 'White with the pattern is the winner.' He stuck the winning shirt on quickly. 'Why are you looking at that time travel junk?'

'I'm interested in the concept.'

'Oh right, are you turning into a geek?'

PJ swung back towards the computer while James pulled up the jeans that were supposed to compliment his whacky shirt. Information regarding time travel was vague to say the least. He could find nothing that helped the two hour dilemma he had suffered today. James stood at the mirror admiring his great choice of clothing.

'What do you think about time travel?' said PJ, still concentrating on the info being churned up in front of him. James stopped prodding at his hair. He cast a concerned eye at his wee brother. 'Are you taking drugs?'

'Don't be stupid all your life James, take a day off.'

'Good, because I'll knock the living daylights out of you if I ever find out otherwise.'

'I don't take drugs, so shut it.'

James noticed that PJ seemed a bit upset which never happened in their brotherly banter sessions. He knew something was wrong. 'Are you alright wee man?' Playtime was over.

'I wish everybody would stop asking if I'm alright.'

'There's a book in the cupboard. It explains that in order to travel through time, some sort of massive energy or explosion would be required. Unfortunately, the world has never witnessed such a bang.'

'Are you taking drugs?' PJ's joke paved the way for banter to recommence. James finished poking his hair and carried out a final inspection.

'You'd love to be this cool, eh?' PJ didn't hear. He turned off the computer, got up and went to find the book. James rubbed his head as he passed, bringing him out the trance. 'Going to the club tonight?'

PJ lifted the time travel book as he answered, 'Probably.'

'Well, same as usual, don't cramp my style. Remember not to nod off to sleep, there's no telling where you might end up.'

'You should be on the television,' said PJ after a sarcastic chuckle.

'I know.'

'As a comedian, you've got the face, hair, clothes, everything to make people laugh.'

James couldn't help taking another peek in the mirror to make sure he was ready for action. 'Yes! All set.'

At the door he turned to PJ. 'Any messages for your mates? Like, PJ couldn't make it tonight guys, He fell asleep and as we speak, has met up with the Russian bob sleigh team for winter training.' Not waiting on an answer, James banged the door closed and laughed all the way downstairs. Fumbling through the pages of Time and Travel, PJ found the smile refusing to leave his lips. He couldn't help but see the funny side of James' light- hearted insult. He needed to concentrate.

Harness the power, blah blah, bends one place to another, blah blah, universal explosions, blah blah. The final chapter ended with:

Travelling through time seems to be an impossibility at this time. Will it ever be achievable? We'll see. Why am I being haunted by these two words? We'll see, we'll see what? PJ lay back on the bed.

Witchwood forest flashed before his eyes. Mr Milne and Mrs Muir laughed as if teasing him. Filling in the gaps of today's events seemed impossible. More effort meant less memory. Thin red lines organised themselves on the radio clock letting him know the time was seven fifteen. He sat the book on the bedside cabinet. The red glow from the clock highlighted its glossy cover containing an atom bomb exploding amidst various fictitious time machines. PJ picked the book up again hoping for a clue. He flipped it over to reveal the author on the back cover. Edmond A. Perkins smiled proudly up at him. How can someone sit and write a book that finishes with I don't really know, thought PJ, chucking Time and Travel into the cupboard. A lot of good you've been Dr Perkins. In fact, I bet way back on your family tree there's an ancestor who swore blind that the world was flat.

Warm spray from the shower massaged PJ's tired skin. He rubbed shampoo onto his scalp in a manner of seeking a miracle cure for memory loss. Water dressed the screen as he lifted off the showerhead. Not even a rendition of pretty woman relaxed his mind enough to allow recollection. PJ replaced the showerhead and pressed the stop button. Clear, comforting silence followed. He stepped out and wiped himself down, feeling refreshed and almost normal but not quite. Once dressed, PJ went to work on his hair. Ten minutes later he checked out the results in the mirror. Now, that's an outfit! Our James must be colour-blind.

On his way along the top hall he noticed Annie kneeling in her room. 'What are you up to small stuff?'

'I need to finish my picture before uncle Alan picks us up.'

'Going somewhere nice?'

'Bowling!'

'Brilliant! see you later.'

'Bye.'

PJ made his way downstairs wishing he could feel the same as Annie, not a care in the world. Instead he felt a world of problems nestling around his shoulders. In the lounge, dad messed about with his sound system while mum messed about with her hair.

'I'm heading to the club!' His exclamation brought great interest from them. Dad pressed the pause button on his hi-fi causing an uncomfortable silence. PJ suddenly felt as if he was leaving home on his first solo journey to school.

'Don't be late,' said mum followed by, 'Come home with James,' from dad. PJ couldn't be bothered explaining to dad how hard the slap would be if he wandered over to James at closing time, waiting to be taken home. 'I'll not be late and I'll come home with James, ok.'

'Have a nice night son,' they replied in unison.

PJ smiled, feeling secure in their concern but also felt uncertainty brewing up again. It brandished an unhappy stick at his lack of memory. 'Bye!'

He set off for Brannigans, unsure.

Chapter 5

Coarse cloud had the last laugh as usual. Shadow cast itself upon rooftops and over pavements. The evening sun glinted off windows here and there along Springfield Place as a reminder of its refusal to take leave just yet. PJ blinked during these occasional glares. His thoughts had already turned to Brannigans. A pay as you play music machine attracted the older teenagers who congregated amidst drink merry adults. This area which contained a few pool tables and a bar is where James and friends hung out.

PJ loved Brannigans on a Saturday night. He produced his membership card and proceeded up a carpeted staircase to the bar area. All round sound overhead pumped out the latest music on offer, delightfully corresponding with the four large LCD screens mounted on each wall. PJ entered the busy bar. James acknowledged his arrival with a cool nod of the head. This indicated, hi, go play with the wee guys. PJ laughed as he wandered over to his own crowd at the other end, head nodding to the beat of the Killers, Mr Brightside.

'Alright guys,' said PJ mixing with the bunch. A few sniggers were among the greetings returned. He ignored the jibes and turned to Joe.

'So, what's happening?'

'Not much, but it's still early. There's four six out of tens, two sevens and an eight over in the corner, all spoken for.' Replied Joe. PJ took a look at the eight out of ten 'Nah, she's only a seven. Sid Savage arrived back from the bar and handed PJ a glass of coke. 'Here you go mate, what happened to you today?' PJ tried to answer but was cut off by Joe. Leave it Sid.'

'I get the hint, why don't we meet up in an hour and you can gee me ma nose back,' laughed Sid strolling off in the direction of the pool tables.

Joe noticed a disturbed look wash over PJ's face as if he was remembering something that would have been better forgotten. 'I've booked a snooker table for eight thirty,' he commented. PJ sipped continuously at his drink before answering. 'Eh, brilliant mate.'

This could be a long night thought Joe. The boys joined in with the ongoing patter, some of which was directed at PJ. Heading to the snooker room came as a relief to both boys.

After an hour of potting balls Joe felt the time was right to prod a bit further. 'Have you remembered anything else yet?' PJ jingled a red, leaving it hanging invitingly over the middle pocket. He straightened up and answered, 'Nope.'

Joe potted the easy red then a few more. He sent the blue ball bouncing off three cushions, hitting the black into the top pocket. 'Are you sure you want to remember?'

'Nope!'

The table light annoyingly flashed overhead. This being the kind signal from the bar to let them know time is up. PJ started emptying balls from pockets, sending them up the table in an untidy fashion. Joe could see that PJ harboured deep thoughts while replacing the cues.

'I think you should tell your mum and dad about today,' said Joe.

'Great idea mate but tell them what exactly?'

'Good point.'

After handing the tray of balls over to Susie, a dark haired nine out of ten behind the bar, they disagreed on who had received the biggest smile. Both came to the conclusion that she was only doing her job as she returned to conversation with a muscle bound giant wearing one of those, hey, I do the weights, tee-shirts.

'Her nose is a bit big.'

'Aye, she's only an eight.'

Back among their friends PJ found it hard to relax, waiting to become the source of the group's laughter at any minute. Joe stood silent, smiling, but also aware. Usually PJ and Joe were at the centre of these talk nonsense sessions. Not even a conversation regarding how good Amanda Simpson looked, running around the athletic track on Tuesday could bring them back on line. Joe became steadily more worried about PJ who looked as if he was sliding into a trance.

'Well, what do you call it then?' enquired Andy Magee.

'What?' asked PJ, coming out of his daydream.

'Rab!' laughed Andy. This caused an inquisitive look to come over PJ's face. He glanced around the crowd then back to Andy. 'What?'

'Rab, that's what you call half a rabbit.'

'Oh, right,' answered PJ realising he'd been slow to getting a joke. He quickly made amends by adding 'You could also call it, bit.'

Sid Savage broke the sudden silence by spraying a mouth full of drink over Stuart Fraser which added to the following laughter. Joe breathed a sigh of relief, sure PJ's one liner would go down like a hot brick into icy water.

It was at this precise moment that Joe first laid eyes on Sarah Timmons. Standing up on a raised area of the bar only twenty feet away, she looked a fine picture. Golden blond hair fell neatly down over perfect cheekbones. Even in the dim light, Joe witnessed piercing blue eyes.

This girl had a smile that made bar girl Susie look like plain Jane, or at least no more than an eight. He'd seen his first ten out of ten. Joe turned to PJ feeling the need to share such a find.

This is when he realised the unimaginable. After checking a couple of times just to be sure, he checked again. The gorgeous girl posed as if in the middle of a photo shoot for Littlewoods catalogue, smiling while holding a tall glass in her right hand. Light danced around the glass, enhancing an already radiating glow. She could sell anything from tents to teapots. Joe accepted the concept. What he found hard to believe was that the cameraman appeared to be PJ. She now leant casually against a pool table as a younger boy took his shot.

'Mate,' whispered Joe. PJ seemed to have forgotten all his problems for now. He and Sid were having a good gab about their own experiences of viewing the athletic Amanda Simpson. 'PJ!' Joe nudged him this time.

'What's up?' smiled PJ?

Joe regained some composure and pulled PJ away from the crowd. 'Promise me that you won't suddenly turn round or do anything stupid if I tell you something.'

'Are you alright? Ok I promise.'

Joe nodded his head then began. 'Right, there's a wee guy playing pool up on table nine and he's rubbish.'

'Is it not supposed to be me who is having a mental breakdown?' laughed PJ.

'Shut it and listen, the wee guy is with a stunner of a girl, don't look around.' Joe managed to get the last part out just as PJ almost swung round.

'Is there a point to all this Joe?'

'She's smiling at you.'

PJ nearly broke his neck turning to look at the girl, who coolly and briefly met his glance before gliding gracefully around the table. She leant over like a professional, winking at PJ before taking her shot.

PJ grabbed Joe by the arm, 'She just winked at me.'

'You're right, look mate no offence but why is a babe like that winking at you?'

'None taken, I don't know but who cares.'

'Go up and speak to her.'

'And say what?' PJ started to feel hesitant. 'The girl just winked at you. Surely you don't need a printed invitation.' The crowd gathered around them. One of the guys had brought drinks, followed by the usual, are you two ever going to venture into your pockets among other derogatory teenage insults. PJ's late arrival to the game caused some interest. Big Stevie Dunn said, 'The boys are all going to chip in and buy a dog leash to get you to the game on time.' PJ laughed and replied 'Brilliant idea big man, once they get me to the game we can put it on you to stop you wandering offside.' Stevie joined in with the outburst of laughter, deciding it would be wise to just leave the matter be. The gang dispersed once again to their various areas of amusement leaving PJ and Joe to return interest towards table nine.

'She's gone!' declared an almost distraught PJ.

Darkness from the now unlit table light scattered shadow to intimidate the encasing brightness of surrounding tables.

'Look for her,' motioned PJ, pushing Joe towards the snooker room.

Meatloaf belted out Bat out of hell on the overhead screens. The big man sang as if his life depended on the performance. PJ stood in the lounge, cradling an uncomfortable thought that this mysterious girl held considerable importance to his own life.

Over behind the bar, muscle man had gone. Susie polished a glass before placing it carefully onto the mirror backed gantry shelf. She paused, momentarily catching a glimpse of herself. Susie was happy with the reflection smiling back. Deep down, the bar girl knew she merited at least a nine out of ten.

PJ continued his search of the bar. Two young lovers sipped cocktails while gazing lovingly into each others eyes. He quickly turned away before the urge to throw up became overwhelming. It was no use. The girl of his dreams had winked and gone. Joe returned from his seek out mission wearing a teasing smug look about him.

'Fancy one wee last game of snooker? Table four is free.'

'Who cares,' answered PJ hoping for better news.

'That girl you fancy might, she's on table three.'

'Joe, you're a genius!'

After a quick trip to collect the tray of balls from Susie, they were on their way for one last game of snooker. 'Remember, when we go in here, be cool,' whispered Joe.

'I'm cool,' replied PJ using his shoulder to open the heavy glass door. It closed slowly behind them, killing off any remainder of bar music. Light also ebbed away with the sound, leaving the typical dull silence of a snooker hall. Occasional conversation and sharp clicks of balls being hit added to the bland atmosphere.

'There she is,' stated a slightly over exited PJ, too loud.

'Is that supposed to be you being cool?' laughed Joe.

'I'm cool,' insisted PJ. He tried with great effort not to stare in the direction of table three. Joe set the balls up while PJ pretended to pick some good cues.

'My break,' said Joe.

'Whatever,' answered PJ, stealing a glance at the girl. She was leaning over eyeing up a shot, hair shimmering down both shoulders. Joe found the situation amusing. It had never been so easy to beat his mate. PJ spent another ten minutes of pointless snooker playing, waiting for an opportunity to speak to her. Now was the chance. They came together while walking round their tables. He built up courage to speak but the girl beat him to it.

'Hi, I'm Sarah.'

Eye contact with her caused the little confidence he had to dwindle rapidly. Eventually, his lips stopped shaking. This allowed him to muster up, 'Alright.'

'Fine, this is my brother Alex,' replied Sarah as the youngster approached them. He nodded to the boy, who looked about fourteen.

'That's Joe,' said PJ, indicating with another head movement towards his mate.

'Hi Joe, what's your friends name?' laughed Sarah.

'PJ, I'm afraid he's a bit shy.'

PJ felt the twangs of anger flush his cheeks red. He wasn't sure who to slap first, Joe or himself. At least the embarrassment had returned some confidence. Sarah smiled. 'Let's start again. My name is Sarah Timmons and this is my brother Alexander.'

'Alright wee man,' said PJ rubbing the youngster's head in the same annoying manner that James does to him.

'Call me Alex,' insisted the boy, flattening his hair back down.

PJ continued, 'I'm Paul Joseph O'Hare. This is Joseph Watson.'

It was almost closing time at Brannigans. One by one, lights flickered out. By ten forty, they were alone in the large gloomy hall. PJ found it a bit easier talking to Sarah but felt weak at the knees if he stared at her for too long. 'I haven't seen you in here before,' he said.

'Were staying with my aunt in Haystone Rd' answered Sarah. Both table lights flickered.

'Time up,' said Joe. They filled their trays, left the quiet dull hall and headed back into the full blown buzz of the lounge. At the bar, Susie smiled efficiently as ever. PJ handed over his tray. She didn't look quite the same now that

Sarah stood next to him. Joe obviously thought differently, barging to the front and insisting on paying. 'I'll get both tables,' he said casually. I wonder who he's trying to impress, thought PJ

They exited Brannigans before being spied by their mates. Outside had been transformed by the departure of sunlight. Its replacement, mostly neon, invited passers-by to eat Chinese, Indian, burgers, anything you fancy. The average person could put on six pounds simply by walking home from a club at night. It wasn't until they crossed Main St into Kings Avenue with only a few lamp posts offering false light, that the night sky became more apparent. A golden moon took pride of place, set picturesquely among tiny bright little dots. The sparkling arcade of beauty was visible to all who bothered peering above ' A free bag of prawn crackers when you spend a tenner' sign.

'It's a lovely night!' exclaimed Sarah. PJ turned to her then in the direction she was looking, which was up. 'Yeh, it sure is,' he agreed. They wandered towards home chatting about this and that.

'What do you get up to on Sundays?' enquired PJ, hoping the girl would say, 'Whatever you want.'

Sarah smiled, 'Different things.'

PJ hoped for a more convincing answer. He now had only two streets left in which to ask her out.

Desperation grew as the group turned into Birch Court. Young Alex informed them that Haystone Rd was just around the corner. PJ let frustration get the better of him. 'No kidding sprout, you don't need to tell us where it is, we live here.'

Alex smiled at PJ, who tried to turn attention back to Sarah but instead, found himself transfixed by a devious grin that drew him into an unwanted staring competition. Words were being said somewhere. Meaningless sentences interrupted at random by weird sounding laughter. Joe whispered something into his ear but it unimportantly mingled with everything else until all simply turned to noise. Alex's eyes became magnets. He felt drawn towards them as if a zoom lens had suddenly taken over his vision, inviting him to take a closer look.
Somewhere in his mind, he catapulted forward, catching
a glimpse of the wicked smile and two wide shining eyes of Alex as he flew past.

Thick, curling, misty cloud lay ahead. PJ hurtled towards it. Every intake of air became an exhilarating pleasure, lifting him faster and further. The cloud thinned away. Faces now appeared, some he recognised, others were strangers. Nothing could be certain at this speed. They spoke while passing but their voices blended into the noisy wind. Eventually, PJ had to lower his head, beginning to lose the battle with the oncoming wind. Unaware of his reduction of speed and altitude, he gazed below at Coalbridge. Fields lay in beds of different shaded little green squares, separated by thin brown lines. A feeling of total freedom filled him as he floated over his hometown.

As cool air refreshed his lungs, vision subsided and memory of the weird day flooded back. Unfortunately, it arrived in a muddled order. Mrs Muir told Bert Wallace exactly what she thought of him. Frankie Milne stood beside them shouting at the top of his voice at anyone who would listen. 'I'm not slow!' he assured all around him. Old Jimmy Henderson walked up to Frankie and slapped him on the face, 'Where's my damn pie you eejit.' The entire Coalbridge Rovers team watched on, while falling about laughing. Rovers captain Stuart Gray exchanged serious words with Bridge East boss Tam McGonnagle. Both cast a threatening look at PJ. Mum and dad came into view, then departed quickly, wearing 'you've let us down again' frowns. PJ blinked, returning his vision to clear blue sky tinged slightly by the sun above.

Down below, thick cloud rose as his speed increased. Memory and thought dwindled away. In the far distance, a black speckle appeared. Growing by the second, it ate into the blue sky until it had become a large black hole. Rovers boss, Bob Kennedy shouted 'PASS!' from somewhere below the cloud. Moments later, the blue sky vanished. PJ was swallowed by the darkness, cascading him into oblivion. He felt himself slowing, then, Dumph!

PJ lay on moist grass. This time though, a moonlit sky met his opening eyes. Joe and Sarah stared at him from behind the hedge of number three Birch court. They looked worried. Alex joined them. He had a look of contentment buried deep within a false concerned face. PJ took a couple of seconds before realising where he was. The evening moisture on the grass soaked into his back.

'What just happened there?' He demanded an answer rather than asking. No one spoke so he picked himself up. Mrs Easton peered through her window blind as PJ rejoined the others on the street. 'That young lad O'Hare dived over our hedge dear.'

'Probably drunk, they're all doing it these days,' replied her husband Brian. Mrs Easton watched them turn into Haystone Rd
'Joseph Watson was there too.'

Mr Easton was barely even listening now that Scotsport had restarted. 'Gone to the dogs, the whole place,' he said.

For the second time today, PJ was aware of doing something stupid. This time, like the last, he still didn't know what or why. Sarah stared at Alex before returning her gaze to PJ. They had almost reached number eleven. 'It's been a few years since we've dived over hedges mate,' commented Joe, not really knowing what else to say.

'Yeh,' agreed PJ, wondering why, if indeed he did, take a run and dive over Mrs Easton's hedges. The only thing he did know was that the two strangers were involved.

They stopped at number eleven. Young Alex avoided eye contact as he headed up the drive, saying 'Bye'!

Joe shouted after him, 'Get some practice at snooker wee man, you're rubbish!'

After saying goodnight to Sarah, Joe started walking slowly back along Haystone Rd. PJ and Sarah were alone at last. Their eyes met briefly before both heads lowered as if something had dropped from above. They followed the invisible excuse to the ground. PJ longed to tell Sarah how the vague artificial light turned her hair to golden silk. Her eyes sparkled like diamonds set in a summer sky. He built up his nerve, and then opted for 'See you later,' much to the amusement of Sarah.

'I better get in, don't worry about Alex, he was only playing around.'

'What do you mean?' enquired PJ.

Sarah leant forward and kissed his cheek. PJ forgot all about Alex. 'Can I see you again?'

'I'm sure you willl' replied Sarah. PJ watched as she disappeared behind the trees of her aunt's driveway, holding his face where Sarah had kissed him. He yelled after her, 'What about tomorrow?'

'We'll see.'

Joe stood at the corner of Haystone Rd, arms outstretched like superman, pretending to dive over a nearby hedge as PJ approached. He let Sarah's kiss fade then returned thought to her comment about Alex only playing around. 'That wee guy made me fly through the air and land in Mrs Easton's garden.'

'Here we go again,' moaned Joe.

Chapter 6

The boys headed out of Birch Court. Joe chatted nervously about nothing in particular, too tired to argue. PJ had spent the last few minutes in a trance trying to remember yet another weird unexplainable event. 'Something's going on.'

'You don't say, Clark,' laughed Joe almost hysterically, knowing a debate was now inevitable.'

'Be serious for a minute Joe.'

'Look, after the day you've had, how can anybody be serious?'

'Trust me mate. I can't explain right now but everything is going to be clear soon.'

'So now you're a fortune teller?'

'No, I just think I'm beginning to remember.' Joe pushed PJ aside and walked on. 'I've had it, go home, and tell your parents their son is a nutter.'

'Sarah said we'll see.'

'Who cares, go home, tell them or I will, tomorrow.'

'Some pal you, eh.'

'See ya.'

'Stuff you!'

PJ wandered on alone. Once home he found the empty house already lit up, courtesy of dad's lamp timer switches. James obviously wasn't through embarrassing himself showing off his dodgy shirt. Within minutes, he was upstairs, stripped and in bed. The quilt had been generously cooled by the breeze filtering through an open window. James might have bad taste in clothing but was brilliant at forward planning. Even places like Scotland require air conditioning now and again.

He lay motionless, trying to make any sense out of this weird Saturday. Cars occasionally passed by, casting a sharp darting light across the dark ceiling. As each light faded, so too, did his concentration. Gradually, PJ emptied the burden from his mind. Another strip of light cascaded over the ceiling but stopped halfway. Car doors thumped shut as the engine hum echoed into the night, then disappeared as gently as its arrival. Mum and dad were home. PJ could hear sleepy groans from Annie being comforted by dad as he carried her up to bed.

Sarah's face appeared before him. Was he sleeping? It didn't matter. She smiled at him. 'We'll see.' Her face drew nearer until he could feel her breath on his chin. Sarah kissed him softly on the lips. 'Goodnight, God bless.' He drifted into a deep sleep, dreaming of nothing as his tired brain rested.

PJ wakened next morning with a startle. Sweat dropped onto his lip, harshly removing any thought of last night's kiss from Sarah. He removed the salty taste with his tongue. Things needed to be sorted today. Memory began rekindling but only of events before and after the forest. PJ dragged himself out of bed, stepping on the colourful shirt belonging to James, as he went for a shower. Fifteen minutes later he was dressed and ready to make good use of his day off.

Mum shouted from downstairs. 'PJ, Joe's here!'

Oh no, he'll tell them thought PJ, running out his room. Mum and Annie sat in the kitchen reading the Sunday papers. They greeted him without raising their heads. 'Want some breakfast?' enquired mum. Annie sniggered at the latest offering of The Broons in the Sunday Post.

'Eh, no thanks, I'll get a bite down at the cafe. Where's dad?'

'He's outside with Joe.' PJ opened the kitchen door to another glorious morning. The whirly full of mum's earlier completed washing gently spun clockwise, encouraged by an ever present fresh breeze. Joe practised keepy ups on the patio chatting to Mr O'Hare who was washing his car. 'Alright, let's go,' said PJ flicking the ball away from Joe.

'Going down the park guys?'

'Yeh, see you later dad.' The boys were on the street in seconds. 'You didn't say anything to my dad, did you?'

'Not yet but you better have a good plan,' replied Joe stealing the ball away from PJ.

Nestling cloud gathered as usual, finding its favourite position in order to submit Coalbridge to sunny, dull instalments. 'I take it we're not going to the park,' added Joe as they headed out of Springfield Place.

'Nope, we'll start off with Sarah's house.'

A little later, PJ sat on the wall opposite number eleven Haystone Rd. Joe emerged from the tree lined drive, face frowning. Not a sign of life inside. The day's plans were to go from bad to worse. Mrs Muir was visiting friends and Mr Milne had taken his family camping. It was now mid-afternoon. Coalbridge enjoyed a long sunny spell due to the cloud having wandered off to annoy some other unlucky sun worshipers. This usually results in UV rays infiltrating family homes, turning normal people into avid gardeners. PJ and Joe were strongly under the influence of fresh cut grass as they made their way to the park. Lawnmowers and hedge trimmers were going berserk.

After the lack of success in finding anyone home, never mind actually solving a part of the puzzle, Joe had agreed to give PJ a bit more time. He didn't want to tell tales on his mate but if PJ persisted on spouting out things like, that wee guy made me fly, then grass, he would. At the park, they joined in with the kick about. Sunday brought no more unusual happenings or results. PJ arrived home exhausted from his run around with the boys. He felt deeply dismayed and frustrated at the lack of not being able to find out anything that could lighten his brain load. He slumped into the comfy two seat couch after dinner wishing the doorbell would ring. He drifted off, into a situation where Sarah entered the lounge, introduced herself then taking PJ aside, explained to him that everything was going to be fine.

After meeting his parents they cuddled up at the pictures watching a great movie.

'Time for bed son!' exclaimed mum, not entirely happy with her sleeping son's facial expressions while lying on the couch. She shook him frantically.

'Yeh mum, I'm knackered,' agreed PJ, making his way off the couch like a zombie.

Up in bed, once sleeping, his mind rewound back to the part where Sarah told him that he was really good looking and she fancied him. His overworked brain went into shut down, after installing one important factor. Sarah Timmons meant something really special to him.

'Goodnight Sarah.'

Monday morning arrived with no option for sunny/ dull, hide and seek. The sun obviously exhausted by a weekend of duelling could do nothing about the thick gathering cloud. Overcast and grey like the sky above, PJ made his way to and from work almost normally.

The week that followed brought only suppressing calmness to the constantly kindled frustration. On the outside PJ masked his troubles well but inside, felt burdened. An invisible force ate into his every idle thought. Keeping busy seemed to be the only defence. Frankie Milne had come into Watson's on Tuesday, tired after his camping trip. PJ made a point of bumping into him while Frankie pondered over which sauce would best accompany his four lamb chops. Mr Milne explained to PJ that he'd run a personal best on Saturday. 'You were going great guns when I saw you in the forest,' remarked PJ, not sure what response this would stir. 'Were you running in the forest too, I can't remember seeing you son,' replied Frankie, tossing a sachet of mint sauce into his trolley.

Mrs Muir proved to be even more unhelpful. She could remember seeing PJ and Mr Milne but not able to recall whether it was in Watson's or the forest, where she had a nasty experience with her dog.

Two more visits to Haystone Rd did nothing to stabilise the steadily going out of control frustration. Life seemed to elude all within the vast sandstone mansion. What had become of this beautiful girl and her annoying brother? Questions needed to be answered but the answers lay inside an empty house. The weekend's game against league leaders and main rivals Bridge West came and went. PJ hadn't played particularly well but he managed to set up the winner for team mate, Stevie Dunn, in a two one victory. Bridge East were now top of the league. After yet another week of sunny then dull weather came Bellway boys club, away from home. PJ and co returned with another three points while Thornton and Bridge west played out a goalless draw. Only now again did PJ allow his mind to wander back to the events of a few weeks ago. Lying in bed on Sunday night, he tried once more to make any sense out of his Thornton time travel episode.

This time though, PJ focused on the probability of confusion. He wasn't sure what time mum came home and handed out his ear bashing. By the time he left for Thornton two hours had past. It's all down to stress. Stress from the dream, then being late for work. Mrs

Muir and Mr Milne were right all along. Nothing actually happened in Witchwood forest. Sarah and Alex Timmons had been real but not to the extent of PJ's first reasoning. Somebody spiked his drink in Brannigans on Saturday night, causing the weird encounter of acting like superman in Birch Court. PJ drifted into a contented sleep. Stress was to blame.

Unfortunately, more stress wasn't far away. After an hour of deep sleep, he became restless. Anxious and sweating, PJ tried to waken up but couldn't. In complete darkness, he felt himself begin to spin, coming to a halt face down, clutching the ground. Before opening his eyes, sense of smell had informed him he was laying on grass. PJ jumped to his feet, eyes wide with surprise. He stood on the lane in Witchwood forest. Everything turned a dusky grey. Breath consuming mist swirled around him. A clearing carved itself, tunnel like, out of the thick moving cloud wall. Into focus came the smiling faces of Sarah and Alex. They seemed close but unreachable. PJ made an attempt to speak but only silent words escaped his lips. Sarah spoke in a strange language, unrecognisable to him. Her smile faded as the mist thickened. He strained his eyes staying focused with the blurry figures of Sarah and Alex who simply blended in and became one inside the grey cloud.

PJ suddenly found himself moving forward towards it without walking. As he made contact, an arm shot out and grabbed his shoulder. 'Sarah, hold on, I've got you!'

Another arm hurtled out of the cloud, slapping him on the face before he got a chance to defend himself.

'Sar…' He tried to call out her name but received another slap.

'PJ are you alright?'

PJ blinked, letting the mist clear. James stood over him wearing that all too familiar concerned look. Even his Homer Simpson boxer shorts looked a bit worried. He let go of his wee brother who gazed around the room as if for the first time. After a few moments PJ had realised he was in another one of these difficult situations. 'Seeing as it's still dark and I'm not late for work, I suppose the question has got to be, did you just slap me there?'

James shook his head in distain. 'PJ you are getting worse, and in answer to your question, aye, I did just slap you.'

PJ rubbed his stinging face while watching his brother dive back into bed. After fumbling into a comfy position, James flicked off the lamp bringing darkness to settle once again into PJ's mind. What was Sarah trying to say? It all seemed so real. He tossed and turned but couldn't get comfortable. Aware of the rustling noise from across the room, James offered some advice. 'Stop mucking about and get to sleep.'

'I can't,' whispered PJ.

'Try harder; it will be beneficial to your health.'

'How can it help my health?'

'Because then I'll not need to get back up and slap you senseless.'

'Very funny' .

'Who's laughing?' moaned James. PJ sat up and glanced into the darkness where James lay. 'Listen, I let you off with the first few slaps but the next one won't be free.'

'Is that right, well I'll bring a pound coin with me when I come over and slap you'!

'Don't bother, the NHS will patch you up for free,' said PJ in his most threatening voice. James let out a tired chuckle and decided it was now time to embarrass his brother into shutting up. 'PJ listen, it's ok for you to fall asleep and instantly become an American wrestler or a member of the Red Arrows sky diving team but when you grab my arm and call me Sarah, you deserve a slap.'

This comment had the desired effect. PJ put the pillow over his head, knowing that James would have a few more things to say before retiring for the night. 'Who is this Sarah anyway?'

PJ squeezed the pillow against his ears but could still hear. 'Is it that looker I saw you with at Brannigans a couple of weeks ago or is she one of your imaginary friends?'

James sensed victory; one last strike would win the battle. 'Drifting off to sleep wee man, maybe Nick Faldo will give you a round of golf?'

Silence joined the darkness at last, after James adjusted to final comfortable position. PJ joined his brother in the land of nod a minute later. As he fell into a deep sleep, Sarah's smiling face appeared before him. PJ had the same weird reoccurring dream throughout the next week. Each morning he awakened feeling miserable.

Thursday morning was his day off this week. He wakened a little later than usual but just as miffed. At least James hadn't needed to intervene with last night's dream. PJ had found himself amidst thick cloud unable to pull Sarah free. When he awoke, James remained sleeping. Unfortunately on Tuesday night his brother roused him from sleep with a pillow on the napper. All things considered, this still faired better than Monday night's rude awakening.

In the middle of PJ's scary nightmare, he tried to pull Sarah free from the cloud when a rock shot through the mist and hit him on the head. Although it was only a dream, he felt pain as if something really had smacked him. After wakening and sitting up he noticed a tennis ball on his bed. James waited until gaining eye contact before stating that the next object to head in PJ's direction was the baseball bat. 'Shut it and get to sleep.'

After a quick glance around his bed and the surrounding floor which were clear, PJ could only assume that his antics hadn't wakened James, whose bed was empty and neatly made. PJ lay back down and listened to Thursday morning through the open window. Motionless, he gazed out at a sky of light blue peppered here and there with the usual cloud. A fresh breeze filtered into the room gently caressing the vertical blinds as it entered. Slow continuous movement added to the calm quiet peace. Apart from the birds of course, who were ranting and raving just outside his window. It wouldn't be so annoying thought PJ, if you knew what they were actually saying to each other. Are they really singing in harmonic bliss or more likely threatening one another? 'That's ma bread in number nine'. 'Oi! Blackbird, git yir beak aff ma worm!' 'Hi Sally, nice set of wings!'

PJ dragged himself out of bed and slammed the window closed before getting dressed.

Joe also lay awake in bed. His plans were a little more in place than PJ's. Unknown to his mate, Joe had been visiting Haystone Rd on a daily basis in order to put some reasoning behind PJ's strange behaviour. If he could get someone home maybe a simple explanation would eliminate these two strangers from the problem. First things first though. Joe would get dressed, eat breakfast then pop into the shop to see if Dad needed a hand. As usual, Jack had matters under control but Joe preferred justifying the, And Son, part of the business.

'Go and enjoy your day off,' smiled Jack, while fingering through a handful of receipts from the local fruit and veg supplier. 'Old git,' he added.

'Who?' asked Joe, already half way out the door.

'Bill Travis has tried to do me out of three bags of spuds again!'

'You've got to admit at least he makes an effort. See you later.'

'See ya, old git.'

Next on the agenda was Haystone Rd. This procedure had involved sitting on the wall opposite number eleven for five minutes. Go up to the door, chap, wait, then return to the wall for another five minutes. All week Joe had carried out the routine with the same outcome, failure. Today he opted for a more direct approach. He crunched over the driveway pebbles onto a path that led to the large oak stained door.

Joe thumped the brass knocker against its mirror like plate, then strained his eyes peering through an oval shaped multi coloured glass panel. He viewed the lifeless hallway in various shades of green and yellow. No use, right, round the back. Joe followed the path around till it stopped at a high wooden fence. Slipping his hand through a curved slot in the gate, he clicked a metal latch up and pushed it open. He continued round to the rear of the property.

The garden was huge. A large granite fountain sat in the centre of recently cut bowling green grass. Water sprinkled from the top of a small figure standing on the odd shaped lump of stone. Joe turned his attention to the massive sandstone house which appeared cold and dull on the inside. Not giving in to frustration he spied an inviting drainpipe and decided on a closer inspection. Taking a foothold on the upstairs window sill, Joe edged over for a peek inside. 'Hi Joe,' came a voice from below. Alex smiled as the intruder slipped before managing to take hold of the drainpipe.

'Have you lost something?'

This isn't happening thought Joe, too embarrassed to look down. He began his descent. Alex watched on obviously enjoying the situation. Once at a safe height, Joe dropped to the ground. 'Erh, alright Alex?' asked Joe feebly

'Yeh! Not too bad. Why were you up there mate?'

Joe bottled it at once, already feeling too stupid to confront Alex about PJ and Witchwood Forest and especially the possibility of being laughed at if he dared mention the fact that his friend seems to have lost two hours, a few weeks ago. All he could think of was 'I'm looking for PJ, have you seen him?'

'No,' answered Alex in a smug, smiling voice.

'He's been trying to get in touch with Sarah, so I thought he might be here.'

'Where, in my aunts room?' laughed Alex.

'Sorry, I don't make a habit of climbing up people's drainpipes,' replied Joe.

'We had to go away for a while, want to pop in and say hello to Sarah. Aunt Anna might know if PJ has been over today.'

Joe thought about the invitation for a few seconds then agreed. At least an opportunity of finding out something must be better than explaining to PJ that he's been hovering around the mysterious house for almost a week, only to be caught climbing the drainpipe and asked to leave, pending a court appearance.

'Yeh, thanks for your help,' offered Joe as he followed Alex in the back door, resisting an overwhelming urge to slap the wee guy from behind.

Chapter 7

Once inside the previously lifeless house, Joe noticed how vibrantly homely it now appeared. Alex led him through the kitchen into a high ceiling well furnished lounge.

'Hello young man, my name is Anna,' stated the elderly lady, hand outstretched.

'I'm Joseph Watson, pleased to meet you,' replied Joe, shaking her hand. Anna was small; fresh faced and had a warm glowing smile. She must be the mother of Mary Poppins thought Joe as he accepted her invitation to sit.

'So, are you boys doing anything interesting today?'

Joe looked at Alex for help. After a small spell of prolonged smugness, he obliged. 'I met Joe at Brannigans a few weeks ago and he challenged me to a game of football on the computer.'

Joe nodded in agreement while trying to remove the look of bewilderment on his face.

'Computers are ruining the world,' said Anna watching the boys making their exit from the lounge. Joe wanted to agree with the old lady and escape but his young inquisitive mind opted for 'How?'

'Well,' continued Anna, 'People have been surviving on this planet for thousands of years, spreading across the world looking for their own space.'

At this stage Joe became intrigued. Alex waited patiently as his football opponent asked Anna another question. 'So?'

'So, computers are allowing Tom, Dick and Harry to know each other's business at the touch of a button. Things were bad enough before this opportunity.'

'So?'

'There would be no problem if Tom could get on with Harry but they don't always, do they.'

'True.'

'Story of the world'! Tom, Dick and Harry meet up. After becoming friends they fall out. Sooner or later poor Dick gets caught in the middle.'

Joe narrowed his eyes and smiled, not really knowing what else to do. Alex came to the rescue once again. 'Spot on as usual Aunt Anna, right Joe let's go.'

'Try a game of chess,' suggested Anna as Joe followed Alex out the lounge.

'I take it your aunt was having a laugh there,' commented Joe,

'No,' replied Alex.

They made their way up a wide carpeted spiral staircase. Wall pictures set in thick brass frames lined the way. Joe took hold of the highly polished hand rail. Each footstep sunk invitingly into the velvety green pile. He checked out the artwork while climbing the stairs. Pictures of great battles and calm landscapes hung beside portraits of proud, happy and sad faces. One painting in particular caught his attention. It featured a younger version of Sarah and Alex, dressed in weird, old fashioned clothing. 'When did you get this one done?' asked Joe, pointing at the portrait.

'Erh, ages ago,' replied Alex. More pictures awaited viewing on the top hall; some of them seemed to intimidate Joe as he passed. 'This one's mine,' said Alex pushing the door open.

In sharp contrast to the rather regal styled hallway, this bedroom looked completely like a young teenager's should. A few items of dirty clothing lay around the floor. Posters of Coalbridge Rovers and Christina Aguilera among others decorated the walls.

'You've got good taste pal,' admitted Joe while Alex flicked the TV screen into life. He clicked onto FIFA and handed a controller to Joe. 'Now you're talking, here we go.'

'Are you ready to taste defeat?' smiled Alex.

'Aye right, give it your best shot.'

PJ wandered around Watson and sons searching for a familiar face that could maybe lead to the whereabouts of Joe, who hadn't answered any texts today.

'Have you tried the park?' asked a slightly worried Jack Watson

'Not yet, but that's where he'll be,' replied PJ in an attempt to pacify his boss.

Back on the street PJ glanced through his contact list. Obviously the first place he looked was the park. Mr Watson didn't need to know this fact just yet.

'Victory!' shouted Joe.

'That's only six-five!'

'To me'!

Anna appeared in the doorway holding a silver tray containing two glasses of sparkling lemonade and a plate full of sandwiches. She placed the tray gently beside the boys. 'Is that your new game?' she asked Alex. '

Yeh,' he replied.

'Looks the same as the last one but I'm sure you'll enjoy it.'

'Sure will.'

Anna departed the room shaking her head. 'Ruin the world they will.'

'Your aunt doesn't think much of modern technology,' exclaimed Joe.

'Nope'! 'My kick off'!

PJ had been everywhere in search of Joe. His trail brought him back to the park.

'He probably went off with big Stu or Arty, we're a man down, fancy a game?' said Sid Savage.

'Why not," decided PJ.

'Foul'! yelled Alex.

'Never'! Tell your wee guy to get up and stop acting like a wimp.'

Sarah sat at a dressing table checking out her reflexion as she brushed golden blond hair away from her face. Amused at the sound of activity in the next room, she smiled as the boys argued and insulted each other. Terminology consisted of, cheat, loser and many other useful adjectives.

'No way'! I want a replay,' demanded Alex.

'Get more practice before you play the champ wee man.'

Sarah popped her head into the room. 'Hi Joe, my brother isn't a very good loser.'

'Rubbish, my controller's not working properly," insisted Alex.

'Mine is working brilliant.' Joe turned to Sarah. 'Alright'?

Alex tossed the controller onto the bed. 'Get you next time.'

'Practise'!

'How is PJ?' remarked Sarah.

Joe didn't want a confrontation but it seemed unavoidable. After all, answers were the reason he decided to climb a drainpipe. Alex and Sarah appeared to be signalling to each other in a secretive manner thinking their actions were unseen to him. It was time for a few questions.

'You might think I've lost the plot, but here goes anyway. PJ thinks that you two caused him to be late for our football game a few weeks ago. I don't mean ten or fifteen minutes. It's more a case of going missing for two hours. Any idea what he's talking about?'

An uncomfortable silence fell upon the bedroom. Sarah and Alex exchanged more serious glances before Sarah waved a hand in front of Joe's face, instantly putting him into a hypnotic trance. He stared at the empty space where Sarah had been standing.

'Keep Joe occupied until I speak to Aunt Anna. Don't let him leave.' Sarah issued her instructions then brought Joe out of the trance with another quick wave of her hand.

'Right then, I better get over to the park,' stated Joe, oblivious to Sarah's hypnotics and the unanswered question.

'Have a look at some of the pictures in the hall before you go,' said Alex, leading him out the bedroom. Sarah smiled and headed downstairs to inform Anna that the time for explanation had arrived.

PJ lay on the grass, game over. Some of the guys were returning with various cold drinks. A cool can of irn bru was thrown at him. He placed it on his forehead and cheeks before quenching his thirst. Stuart Fraser arrived with the juice buyers. He bumped down next to PJ. 'Have you seen Joe today mate?'

'Naw, I've been over at my gran's all day,' replied Stu, letting himself fall back onto the warm grass. 'This is the life, eh,' he added, staring up at a clear blue sky. The clouds would probably be back soon with reinforcements.

Alex stopped at a wall painting on the mid landing. Joe studied the detail. An elderly silver haired gentleman stood knee deep in a flowing stream, fishing rod in mid motion overhead. His shimmering shadow rippled across the water, almost to the opposite side. The banks of the stream gently rose up to meet lush green hills sprinkled with dots of yellow and purple. The source of the flowing water was a magnificent waterfall in the far distance. Dark patches of forest and woodland bordered the painting. Sunlight drenched a golden haze over everything.

'He looks a cool old dude.'

'Yeh he is, do you want to meet him?' replied Alex.

'Why, is he coming to visit?'

'Sort of.'

Alex touched the back of Joes head. It felt like a bolt of lightning, knocking him forward. A feeling of spending time somewhere with no recollection of when sank overwhelmingly into his mind. Darkness subdued him. Sound and smell took over. Fresh air coated in country scent that Joe could recall from family away days invaded his senses. Rushing water whispered below him.

'Hello young man.'

Joe became aware of two aspects. His eyes were closed and feet wet.

'Jumping like dolphins they are,' added the strange friendly voice.

'Am I having a nervous breakdown?' asked Joe opening his eyes cautiously.

'Pleased to meet you, my name is Angus McEwen.' Bushy white whiskers curled up around the old guy's reddish cheeks. He shook the baffled boy's hand then gave him the fishing rod which began shaking erratically. 'Quick! You've got one.'

PJ sat at the dining table poking and prodding at a plate of bangers and mash. Mum hovered around picking things up, sitting things down. 'Joe's dad phoned a while ago to see if he was here. Did you see him at the park today?' PJ accidentally slammed a link sausage through the mash mountain he had created while answering. 'Erh no, I haven't seen him.'

After a few more minutes of eat a little, carve a little, PJ left his plate lying on the dining table. He sent another text to Joe while heading upstairs. Mrs O'Hare shook her head with worry as she lifted the half eaten dinner, PJ never left any bangers and mash.

Alex appeared behind Joe who had the rod in one hand and a giant pink salmon in the other. 'Look at this beauty I just caught.' He held his trophy aloft.

'Well done mate, time to go.'

Joe handed his prize to Angus then turned back to Alex. 'I think its time to tell me why I'm standing in a river.' Joe tried to speak again but couldn't. Keeping his eyes open became impossible as a sudden wind gathered around him. Angus shouted, 'See you tonight young man.' Then all sight and sound dissipated leaving Joe suspended in a silent limbo. Next came a feeling of being pulled backwards by an invisible bungee rope. When the sensation ended he opened his eyes to find himself staring at Angus. The old man smiled from the confines of his glossy enclosure holding the fish Joe had caught. 'Wow!'

Once he finally managed to break his gaze from the painting Alex took him by the arm.

'We need to talk.' Sarah and Anna stood at the bottom of the staircase, both faces deep in concerned thought. 'Let's all have a nice cup of tea and a chat,' said Anna.

Ten minutes later Joe sat uncomfortably in the lounge. Anna reached forward almost sticking a tray of cakes into his face. 'Have another,' she insisted. Joe laughed which came out as a nervous rant. 'Are those windows double glazed?' he asked.

'Why?' said Anna.

'Because I'm thinking about diving through it to get away from you lunatics.'

Alex went into a fit of giggles at Joe's comment. Sarah seemed a bit more reserved. Anna just smiled her warm reassuring smile. 'We are telling you the truth dear.'

Joe got to his feet 'So, I'm not drunk or drugged and you lot are angels.'

'Yes.' stated the other three. Joe ran for the door but before he could reach it Anna appeared in front of him. He spun around to where she stood previously, then back to meet her honest smile. 'Wow!'

Anna placed a hand gently on his head. 'I'm sorry we've had to involve you but due to your friendship with PJ it seems imperative to putting things right.'

'What things?'

'Everything will become clear in good time dear.'

Joe nodded his head in agreement. An abnormal calmness had come over him, induced by Anna's touch. He no longer felt overwhelmed by the news. Sarah came into focus. 'Thanks for offering to help.' Only then did Joe realise he was sitting down. It never even bothered him how or when he got back to the chair. 'No probs.' Anna gave some instructions to Joe while he gradually returned to normal. She finished off by urging him to act normal. PJ mustn't be told anything regarding angels until dinner on Saturday night which they were both invited to. 'Think you'll be able to act normal?' smiled Alex. 'Shut it, you're not very good at fifa for an angel!'

'I let you win!'

After promising to stick to his instructions Joe strolled along Haystone Rd feeling more relaxed than he'd been in his entire life. Angels eh, who'd have thought? I wonder what that old gal did to me when she touched my head. I could do with a pat on the napper once a day off her. Anna also admitted to blocking his calls today, thus no contact from PJ. Joe's first instruction was to text him once home explaining that his battery died. Then mention bumping into Alex and so forth. Joe wandered to the corner of Willowbrae Gardens muttering his thoughts out loud.

PJ arrived at the same corner going so fast he almost knocked Joe over a fence. 'Wow, chill dude, you nearly took me out there,' stated Joe far too calmly.

'Chill, dude, are you just out of Sarah's house there?'

'Do I detect a wee bit of jealousy mate?'
PJ automatically went into defensive mode. 'Naw, I'm asking what you've been up to all day. You're Dad phoned our house to see if you were with me.'

'Right calm down, walk this way and I'll explain today's events.'
PJ followed Joe along Willowbrae Gardens as his mate described in detail how he had accidentally bumped into Alex while heading for football at the park. One thing led to another ending up with the wee annoying guy challenging him to a game of fifa at his house, which obviously Joe had won. The battery in his phone was low so he turned the phone off.

'Did you see her?' said PJ
'Who'?

'Who do you think?'

Joe laughed 'If you mean the blonde haired girl you're daft about, I spoke to her on the way out.'

PJ didn't reply at first. He concentrated on remaining cool. After a few steps of controlled emotion his eagerness got the better of him. 'Did she say anything about me?'

'She mentioned you.'

'What did she say?' begged PJ, self-control gone.

'Sarah asked me to apologise for her suddenly having to go away on family business and she's looking forward to seeing you on Saturday night at her house for dinner.'

'No way!'

'Way!'

Joe carried on with his explanation, most of which not being exactly true. In fact had he suffered the same affliction as Pinocchio, would be in danger of tripping over his own nose any second now. PJ wouldn't have heard anyway. Saturday night planning was already underway.

I need to make a good impression, need a good opening line. Joe continued bending the truth slightly. It came over to PJ as blah! Blah!

Friday arrived and went almost unnoticed. PJ spent most of it in a daze while working on his entrance speech to Sarah. Hi, hello, how are you doing? Definitely more work required. So far he sounded like a reject James Bond. Throughout the day furniture got bumped into and food was dropped in a Hansel and Gretel type trail wherever PJ went around the house. He ignored family members while wandering about talking to himself. James noticed all the signs. 'I think PJ's in love.'

Chapter 8

Saturday morning launched into PJ's bedroom in fine fashion. Sunlight swept across the ceiling and slapped his face with a firm reminder that today is the big day. Panic set in momentarily until a glance at the clock let him know it was only ten-fourteen. After a pulsating heartbeat had gradually returned to normal he swung his legs onto the floor and sat up.

Straight ahead lay his awkwardly inquisitive brother. 'Alright?' smiled James.

'Of course I'm alright, it's my day off,' replied PJ in between yawns.

'What are you getting up to the day then?'

PJ could sense motive behind his brother's stupid smile and sudden great interest. Defensive mode was required. 'There's no game on so we'll probably head down to the park.'

'Are you meeting up with your girlfriend?' asked James hoping for a bit of useful conversation.

'What girlfriend?'

'Aye right,' laughed James chucking a pillow at his smug little brother.

PJ showered, dressed then went through the usual routine of poking and prodding at his hair until cool untidy look had been achieved. Excitement of finally seeing Sarah again overwhelmed him as he tried to carry out a normal Saturday procedure. Most of the day consisted of him smiling at everyone. He returned from the park and showered again before dinner, a requirement after kicking a ball around for a couple of hours. James watched on as PJ polished off a full plate of stovies and two buttered plain outsiders, managing to chew while maintaining the fixed smile. Once his brother had left the table James commented to mum, 'Our PJ has definitely got a wee bird.'

Upstairs, PJ opened his wardrobe door like a man on a mission. After trying a few variations he eventually opted for the plain white shirt to show off his tan. The mirror tried its best to highlight the pinkie whiteness but the boy saw only glowing colour. 'I look the part.'

Everything seemed perfect on the way over to Joe's. Grass appeared greener, birds were actually harmonising instead of just making an annoying noise.

'Tell me exactly what she said,' pleaded PJ while the boys entered Haystone Rd.

'The same as I told you yesterday and the day before that. Try and be cool.'

'I'm cool!' Nervous chat continued along to number eleven. Joe unconsciously rubbed his forehead creating a warm sensation that made him feel at ease.

PJ chapped the large brass knocker. 'Oh well, here goes.' The door opened smartly. Anna emerged from the dull hallway into bright evening sunshine. 'Hello Joe and you must be PJ, please come in.'

PJ held back the urge to scream out, 'where is she!' Anna's warm smile was a welcome soother to his ever increasing heartbeat. He got the feeling though, Anna already knew his thoughts. Joe stood back while Anna shook hands with PJ. She placed her other hand on his forehead without him being aware of doing so. 'Let's go through to lounge boys.'

PJ wandered along in front looking instantly relaxed. Joe winked at Anna and jokingly stuck his head forward in a manner of, I know what you just did there, and can I have some please? She touched his head as he walked by. 'Wow, cheers!'

I think you may need that before the evening ends muttered Anna to herself.

Joe had received a top up of 'hey man I'm feeling good' but as PJ made his way along the friendly old fashioned hallway, a notion of discomfort carved its way into his newly relaxed brain. A sickening sensation of an unknown entity registered momentarily among the calmness, then dissipated leaving a burning emptiness

'Third door on the right boys,' said Anna from behind. Her words rescued PJ from his frightening labyrinth of thought.

Sarah and Alex stood at the top of the staircase watching as Anna ushered the boys into the lounge. 'It's time to help him face the music,' said Alex. 'Yeh,' answered Sarah. 'Let's go.'

Anna chatted away about the evening's plans. PJ listened attentively until the door opened. 'Alright guys?' smiled Alex. PJ didn't hear, he only had eyes for the beautiful girl standing next to him.

'Hi,' the word rolled off his tongue easily.

'Hello again. I'm sorry we had to go away so suddenly. I forgot to get your number.'

'It's my fault, I should have given it to you,' replied a starry eyed PJ.

Anna broke the short silence that followed. 'Ahem, shall we go, Angus is waiting.'

The youngsters followed Anna into the hall. PJ and Sarah tagged along behind.

'You look brilliant tonight,' whispered PJ

'Thanks.' Sarah blushed then said 'you don't look bad yourself, does that sunburn not hurt?'

Maybe my tan is still a bit red just now thought PJ as he smiled back 'Eh, not much.'

'Is the dining room upstairs?' mentioned Joe noticing the direction they were heading.

'Sort of,' replied Alex.

They came to a halt half way up. PJ arrived on the wide mid landing last. Alex and Joe stopped behind Anna. Sarah joined them. She beckoned on PJ to do the same. It suddenly appeared dimly lit all around.

'We must hurry,' insisted Anna. PJ quickly shuffled in behind Joe. 'Are we waiting on a bus?' laughed PJ trying to make light of the fact that they all now stood staring at a wall.

'Kind of,' added Alex.

Five wall paintings hung in front of them. Light softly emulated within the centre frame, building up to a bright glow. An unusual noise followed. Sarah took PJ's hand. He smiled at her then returned gaze towards the source of light. The portrait of the old man exploded into colour. 'What the!' PJ never got the chance to finish his sentence. He felt the tightening grip of Sarah before a whirlwind sucked him up. Everything throttled forward. Sparks flew out, coating everyone in a shimmering glitter.

PJ closed his eyes as the rushing wind became too intense. Panic began to settle in and he struggled to breathe. His tight grip to Sarah remained but it couldn't stop the onslaught of loneliness overtaking him.

Before the mayhem turned to terror, a brief whirring sound grew louder then stopped, bringing the proceedings into stark silence. PJ could feel his heart beat uncontrollably, threatening to burst out and make a break for it.

'Exemplifying entry as usual,' said an unusual voice.

PJ opened his eyes as wispy cloud rose, allowing him to focus on the elderly gentleman. A broad smile could be seen below bushy whiskers. His sideburns came down and around almost to meet the moustache. Thick wiry white hair sat in a clump on his head in need of a brush. He wore a brown tweed suit, yellow shirt finished off with a blue and white polka dot bow tie. The friendly character didn't bother using colour coordination when dressing.

Angus had a confident manner about him which suggested he also couldn't care less what anyone else thought regarding his whacky dress sense.

'Angus dear, it's a pleasure as always,' said Anna reaching out to meet the old man's outstretched hand. She carried out the introductions but PJ got the impression that Joe and Angus had met before. 'Erh, no I've never seen the old boy in my life,' whispered Joe in his defence after a quiet elbow in the ribs from PJ.

Angus and Anna led the group along his hallway which resembled Haystone Rd in both decor and wall paintings. Two large doors opened as they approached, leading into the dining room. 'What a pad, eh?' exclaimed Joe. After a quick glance around, PJ agreed.

Impressive it was indeed. Rectangular in shape, a decent game of tennis could be played within. The main feature being a long oak dining table situated in the centre. Fresh white linen dressed the dark oak, emphasised by three candelabras softly flickering golden flame over the silver dinnerware. Seven places were set on the table that could easily dine twenty. Two sparkling chandeliers hung overhead adding crystal light to all below. Wood panelled walls stained in deep mahogany met a high bright white ceiling. More paintings complimented the panelling, much to the delight of Joe who studied each one vigorously as if choosing a holiday destination.

His wandering eye fell on a dark haired girl who posed in front of a beautiful clear blue lake. A fairground scene sat in the background with sunlight shimmering through a big wheel full of tiny smiling people. Below the girl's left elbow were the words, Julie at Inglefoot Fayre. Joe wished he could just skip dinner and head off to this mysterious place, hopefully bumping into the girl with the mesmerising smile on his arrival.

PJ took his seat opposite Sarah. The double doors through which they had entered slowly creaked shut. Behind Sarah, two identical doors were slightly ajar allowing bright light to escape across the ceiling. Four more single doors were set into the wood panelling. He counted another four on the opposite wall. Who would need ten exits out of a dining room? Turning to Sarah he decided to lose his apprehension in her gorgeous smile while trying to keep calm anticipation.

Angus attracted everyone's attention with a well mannered 'Ahem!' 'Thank you ladies and gentlemen. I hoped Simon could join us for our first course but he has unfortunately had to relinquish the prospect of fresh fish. Due to unforseen circumstances which he ensures us are entirely equitable but nevertheless unavoidable.'

'I think we should wait on Simon. I'm sure our young guests could amuse themselves for an hour or so,' motioned Anna.

'Excellent idea, it would be better to dine together,' added Angus.

Before anyone got a chance to respond, Joe asked who the girl was in the picture. He pointed at her as if hypnotised. 'Would you like to meet her?' whispered Alex.

'Is a bear likely to do its business in the woods,' muttered Joe in reply.

'I take it that means yes?'

'It means of course I would you Wally. Is she coming tonight?'

'Not exactly,' said Alex winking at Joe.

'Right, I get it,' Joe winked back. Another one of these shoot through the picture jobs thought Joe as he made his way over to the painting. Julie looked even more beautiful close up. It would be worth flying through oblivion to meet her.

PJ and Sarah wandered around the table to join Alex. Joe continued to stare at the canvas. They all decided that Inglefoot Fayre looked pretty interesting. 'That's Julie at the front,' said Joe pointing at the tanned skinned girl smiling back at them. He braced himself, awaiting the journey, eyes fixed on Julie.

'Shall we go then?' asked Alex.

'Whenever you're ready,' answered Joe, keeping eye contact with the girl. He resembled a skier waiting for the signal to descend a steep slope. PJ tapped his shoulder. Joe turned to see Sarah and Alex standing at an open doorway.

'We use doors to travel when we visit Angus,' replied Alex, just to add a little insult to injury.

Joe looked dumbfounded and totally embarrassed. He straightened up and followed the others out of the dining room. They entered a narrow hallway with no other way out.

'Has anyone heard the old saying, when one door closes another opens,' asked Alex.
PJ and Joe nodded.

'That statement was invented here in this house,' added Alex.

'Is that right?' commented Joe.

'Yes! So will you shut the door?'

Anna and Angus smiled as the door banged shut. 'Youth is such a great gift.'

'Shame it gets wasted on the young,' replied Angus.

Inside the tight hallway, the echo of the door closing faded with Joe saying, 'has anybody heard the saying, he who tries to rip the mince shall receive a worldly slap.'

'I don't think so,' answered Alex.

'That's probably due to the fact that I just invented it a moment ago, so keep it in mind.'

'I'll not forget that one,' laughed Alex while placing a hand on the white wall. Dark lines formed, etching into the smooth surface until a door had been created.

'Cool,' said PJ and Joe together.

Sarah stepped forward gently pushing the door outwards. Fresh air rushed in filling their lungs as wind curled around them then left a calm silence, an equivalent to Anna's touch. They stepped out onto grass, blinking as their eyes became accustomed to the brilliant sunshine. 'Welcome to Inglefoot Fayre!' exclaimed Alex pointing towards the spectacle.

At first sight, Inglefoot Fayre appeared a touch more turbulent than the calming scene hanging in the dining room. Laughter scattered around freely. Shouts and excitable screams could be heard from various rides.

'Where is she?' demanded an anxious Joe.

'Over on the waltzer. C'mon I'll introduce you,' said Alex.

'You're not a bad wee guy,' replied Joe patting his back as they set off.

'I suppose all the rides are free, which one first?' asked PJ, taking Sarah by the hand.

'Let's try the big wheel, we need to have a chat,' replied Sarah.

Sarah spent the next hour being dragged from one ride to another without getting a chance for her chat with PJ. They noticed the others sitting at a picnic area by the waters edge. Alex and Joe were laughing and joking while munching their way through the contents of a basket full of delights. Julie also shared a place on the tartan blanket.

Sarah led PJ over to another readymade picnic blanket. 'I didn't notice this a moment ago,' he stated as they sat. 'Yeh, that's Inglefoot Fayre, full of surprises.'

Anna found it hard to relax in the empty dining room. She stared at the picture of Inglefoot Fayre. Julie had now disappeared from the front. Angus returned and noticed her worried expression. 'Things will turn out fine, you mustn't worry.'

'I'm sure they will,' she agreed.

'Simon will arrive with good news.' Angus had also now lost some of his merry demeanour but tried to mask anxiety.

PJ sat amidst the newly acquired lunchbox still insisting that it wasn't there a minute ago. 'This place is brilliant,' he insisted while polishing off a perfectly warm chicken breast.
Sarah didn't bother trying to convince him to keep some appetite for dinner. At least she now had the chance to explain a few things. 'What can you remember about the experience in the forest a couple of weeks ago?'

PJ didn't answer right away. His mind drifted back to the afternoon in question. He could feel small pieces fit into place. 'I think I remember a voice like yours saying, we'll see, and you must go now,'

Before Sarah got a chance to open her mouth Alex approached. 'Hey you two, fancy a trip to the memory booth?' Joe and Julie strolled behind him.

'C'mon it sounds like a laugh,' added Joe, while pulling PJ to his feet.

'Why not, seeing as I'm standing up now,' said PJ in a sarcastic tone.

Sarah gave him a long meaningful gaze. 'We'll have a talk later.' She took his hand as they followed the group.

Magical memories wait inside. 'Aye right,' said Joe passing a shabby advertisement board. The memory booth was a simple dome shaped tent. An old man stood at the entrance. He handed out large gold coins to eagerly outstretched hands of those entering. The queue snaked along wooden planks until reaching the rough canvas entrance. Once inside, people were transported along a narrow passage courtesy of a conveyer belt before being deposited rather abruptly into yet another passage way.

In the dull light PJ could barely see the walls. After a touch he found they were now inside a brick built construction. Strange having walls in a tent?

Everyone began bumping together as the queue filtered down to single file in the narrowing corridor. An elderly woman operated a silver turnstile up ahead. 'Tokens please, thank you,' she repeated. The bar creaked as it rotated, allowing people to proceed through a slot in the middle of a velvet curtain. PJ waited his turn, handed over the gold coin as Sarah disappeared behind the curtain. He smiled at the old lady then pushed the thick curtain apart and stepped inside. 'Wow! How can all this fit into a tent?'
Joe arrived at his back. 'Wow!'

The memory booth was massive. White walls shone under brilliant sunlight protruding the high glass roof.

'This way please,' instructed a man in a sharp white suit. The group tried to keep up as he turned and walked away.

'This place is like a giant railway station without the tracks or trains,' stated PJ.

'It used to be something along those lines,' answered Alex.

Four long rows of chairs sat back to back stretching over hundreds of feet. They were full of people young and old, sitting as if in a deep trance.

'One day only sir,' said the smartly dressed fast walking gentleman. It sounded like he was insisting rather than asking. 'That's correct,' replied Alex. They made their way through the hustle and bustle of the crowded area. People not seated seemed to be in a hurry to get somewhere. Footsteps clumped in all directions. Sharp suit led them into a small building in the centre of the massive arena. A neon sign flashed on and off above the door. Welcome to the memory booth. 'Enjoy your short stay,' said the man. He bowed quickly then departed.

'What now?' enquired Joe.

'We sit and wait,' answered Alex taking his place on one of the five black chairs against the far wall of the otherwise empty room. The rest did likewise.

No more than a minute had gone by when mist began to seep through the opposite wall. It crept to the middle of the room, rising and thickening until becoming a dense blanket. Then as if by an extractor fan fitted in the ceiling the mist cleared leaving five similar cubicles in place. They resembled those you would have a passport photograph taken in, only a bit more old fashioned. Each booth had a half wooden door at the bottom and a curtain on top

'For anyone who hasn't visited the booth before,' said Alex looking at PJ and Joe. 'This is a simple procedure.' Enter the booth, close the curtain and sit. There will be three buttons on the panel in front of you; green, red and blue. Most people press green which always recalls a good memory. Red can be risky, good or bad. Only go for blue if you wish to remember a bad experience'

'Green for good, red can be risky and blue is bad. No problem, let's do this,' said Joe already on his way to a booth. PJ waited until everyone else had picked their own then entered and swished the curtain shut. As Alex had explained, three buttons were in front of him. Above them, inscribed into the wood, a warning advised to cancel, press the same button.

'Here goes,' whispered PJ pressing the green button. Instantly, a far away feeling of relaxation filled his senses. He found himself singing Christmas carols, snuggling into Dad on the old couch they used to have. An urge to hold on tighter overcame the initial embarrassment of cuddling his Dad. I don't do cuddles with Dad anymore. Emotions told him otherwise. PJ sang his heart out while reliving little Annie's first Christmas eve. A tidal wave of that particular night roller coasted through the cobwebs of a forgotten time. He felt himself hit the button, returning once more to the quiet confides of the empty booth.

Intense worry of needing to get to sleep before Santa arrived, flooded in. He knows when you are sleeping.

PJ snapped out of the trance. 'Wow! That was totally cool.'

Not wasting time he pressed the green button again. The scent of seawater overtook awakened senses. Waves crumbled onto sand, frothing around his ankles. PJ watched on at first then became the young boy splashing around in the water.

'Got you sprout!' PJ shivered as James pulled him from the oncoming waves. Millport was brilliant but the water always felt a little cold. PJ hit the button again letting holiday memories rush in, absorbing each thought until firmly restored back into his long term memory banks.

PJ decided to have one last go. He let the heart lifting thoughts of old settle first then opted for red. 'Why not try risky, I don't think I've got any bad memories.'

The small cubicle became dark. Silence burned fear into his blindness. He hit the button again. It felt like he was being removed from a frightening nightmare. The new info merged and clung like a spiders web onto the newly bestowed happiness just received. PJ wiped cold sweat from his face and left the booth. One by one the others emerged smiling and relaxed apart from Joe who came through the curtain looking like he'd just bumped into the tango man.

'Are you alright mate?' asked PJ.

Joe slung a gaze back into the booth before answering. 'I think so.' He sat down and exhaled a deep breath that sounded like a jet engine in reverse thrust.

'Remember I told you about carrying out an onslaught on a spider moving across my ceiling, one Saturday morning, years ago?'

'Aye, you missed it until the creepy wee thing was right above your head, then you finally made contact. It fell onto your face.' laughed PJ

'That's the very day I'm talking about. Guess what! It just happened again.'

Joe's revelation made everybody laugh. PJ smiled along with the group but didn't mention his own bad experience. Perhaps it was a malfunction in the booth.

'I think we should make our way back now,' suggested Alex.

'They all agreed and headed for the red flashing exit sign that would allow them to take leave from Inglefoot Fayre. Mr bright white suit bowed while holding the door open for the departing guests.

Chapter 9

'Ah! our young guests have arrived with another friend,' said Angus as the group entered the dining room.

'Hi,' replied Julie, blushing slightly. She sat opposite Joe, in front of the picture of Inglefoot Fayre which still displayed the delights on offer, minus the cute girl as its feature.

Once they were seated, idle chat commenced about their adventures at the fayre. PJ told his listeners about learning to swim at Millport and Annie's first Christmas but felt reluctant to reveal anything regarding his last choice in the memory booth.

'Some things are meant to be kept secret,' commented Anna, helping PJ to escape the difficult situation. 'Yeh,' he added.

Angus slid his chair back. Its course sound brought everyone to attention.

'Thanks for your patience. Simon will be joining us shortly,' His latest speech got cut short by an opening door. A tall dark haired man entered. Simon excused himself for being late stressing that it couldn't be avoided. PJ and Joe watched on as the tall guy took his place at the table. He resembled a rocker with his long hair and rough appearance but carried a calm powerful demeanour, camouflaged only when he smiled. Dressed in jeans and tee-shirt, Simon remained standing as Angus introduced him to PJ and Joe. 'You know everyone else,' added Angus.

'I am looking forward to dining with you all this evening but there are a few matters need to be concluded beforehand.' Turning attention solely to Angus, 'Some other guests would like to join us for dinner if you don't mind.' Angus looked a little uncomfortable when saying it would be a pleasure. Silence fell upon the dining room. Joe broke the monotony by asking Simon if he'd ever been in a rock band. The latest guest laughed and replied 'I did a bit of singing a long time ago.'

'You never got a big hit eh?' enquired Joe

'Not exactly.'

Casual conversation began among the group. PJ listened in on Simons chat with Angus and Anna while pretending to be paying attention to Joe. 'I have spoken at length with the council and they have agreed to bring a final decision tonight.' Simon spoke low. Angus and Anna nodded their heads but appeared nervous.

'Why don't you young ones go and amuse yourself again. It appears dinner shall be delayed a little longer.' Said Anna, already on her feet and heading for another door.

'Excellent idea,' added Angus.

Anna stood at the open door like a lollypop lady beckoning oncoming children across a busy road. She shepherded them one by one through the door.

Before Angus could speak, Simon answered his question. 'I am doing all I can at the moment.'

Anna turned as she closed the door 'This is an outrage. The matter should be dealt with by us.'

'I agree,' replied Simon who stared at the glossy dressed dining table. After a brief pause he looked up at Angus and Anna. 'Let's wait for their decision.'

'This young man shall live regardless of the decision,' insisted Angus.

'I am here for that very reason friend,' replied Simon.

'Think they were trying to get rid of us?' laughed Joe as the dining room door slammed behind them, closing the group in yet another narrow white walled hallway. Two new doors began forming on the far wall.

'What's this, a choice?' said PJ eyeing both options. One door had a silver knob handle, the other a large golden lever.

'Any great ideas?' stated Alex. 'Do you like football Julie?' asked Joe.

'I love it!'

'Any chance of maybe going to a European cup final then?' he begged.

'Which year should we go for?' said Alex.

'1967!' answered PJ and Joe together.

'No problem, that's the year a group of local lads, beat a world class team if I'm correct.' Alex opened the gold lever door.

'Dad went to that game in Lisbon with my Granda when he was five. He'd still go see Celtic every week if he wasn't so busy working.'

Indeed, both PJ and Joe's dads were ardent Celtic supporters but encouraged the boys to follow their Town team due to not being able to take them to Celtic games because of work.

All of their team-mates at Bridge East were Coalbridge Rovers fans. Half were also Celtic fans while the others hearts occasionally lay fifteen minutes along the M8 in Govan, home of Rangers FC. Considerable wind-ups often occurred if either team got beaten, such is the west of Scotland creed. This old tradition though, carried patter from both sides of the divide that was second to none. It always ended, sooner or later in laughter. Well, in this part of Coalbridge anyway.

Alex held the door open as Joe and Julie marched through. PJ automatically pursued the footie fanatics only to be jerked back by Sarah.

'We need to talk. Let's go for the other door.' Her friendly appearance seemed to be shrouded in stark insistence.

'I suppose there's no use saying I want to see the football game?'

'You'll get another chance to see it,' replied Sarah taking him into the other doorway.

They had to cover their eyes from blinding sunlight in the newly opened door.

Small crests of snowdrops floated around on an eventual journey's end to a crisp white landscape. Fir trees coated sugar like encircled the border of a frozen lake. Snowflakes dropped sparsely, putting the finishing touches to this winter scene. Families glided around the glass floor. Couples skated hand in hand laughing and showing off. Everything seemed perfect. Only landing snow could have cause for dissatisfaction as lots of silver blades cut and scored their way over the icy surface.

'Well it's not up there with a cup final but it looks alright,' admitted PJ as they headed towards the frozen lake

'Can you skate?' asked Sarah.

'Of course I can, a bit anyway.'

Sarah led him onto the ice, merging with the circling skaters. He was glad they opted for the complimentary jackets and scarves on arrival. After ten minutes she guided him back over to the edge. A step up onto a wooden rim took them to safety from the oncoming skaters

Two young lovers drifted past, smiling at each other in between quick snogs.

PJ looked at Sarah. Long hair strayed messily across her weather-chilled face. It made him forget all about the football. He couldn't quite understand why this beautiful girl was standing next to a normal guy like him. Then again, none of this was exactly normal.

'Let's sit over there,' she said.

'Erh, Yeh.'

Once they were seated on a bench beside the frozen lake Sarah sighed. 'Where do I start?'

PJ didn't answer. He gazed ahead at the laughter and merriment in full flow without really seeing or hearing any of it.

'This whole thing is a mess.'

'How much of a mess are we talking about?' enquired PJ, still staring at the passing skaters.

Sarah spent the next thirty minutes explaining what she and Alex had done in the forest on that particular Saturday. How it had begun as fun then became complicated.

'It sure did, I missed my game by two hours and ended up arriving like a raving lunatic.' PJ seemed pretty calm discussing the matter, considering the circumstances.

A keen young skater tried a high double spin, resulting in a small pile up right in front of them. This eased the growing tension as people picked themselves and others up. Sarah waited until the minor fracas ended before continuing. 'I had to initiate the time lapse.'

'Why?'

Just then, the snogging couple glided by causing a distraction. 'That must take a lot of practise, being able to skate while stuck to each other's faces. Anyway, what's the time lapse?' added PJ.

Sarah appeared to take a great deal of thought before making her next comment.' Do you believe in fate?'

'What are you talking about?' replied PJ becoming more intrigued by the second.

'I mean what is to be, is going to be.'

PJ took in the information, tossed it around a bit then decided he still had no idea what she was talking about. Sarah held his hand. 'We were not supposed to be in the forest on that day but got told to go at the last minute for R and T practise.' PJ consumed the additional info, let it churn around. 'Ok I get it; you've been messing around in some sort of way with this fate thing and got caught.'

Sarah didn't reply. It was her turn to stare at the inhabitants skiing past.

'I knew it. What's the worst they can do to you, they're not going to kill an angel,' laughed PJ, trying to cheer her up.

'I'm not the one in danger.'

Anna refused to sit. She paced the dining room floor, stopping occasionally at the drinks cabinet to fill her Sherry glass. Angus and Simon watched on in silent thought. A loud chap on the door brought them back to reality.

'Our guests have arrived,' said Angus jumping to his feet. After a reassuring glance at Anna and Simon he opened the door. Two men and a middle-aged woman all dressed in conservative black entered. Angus directed the new guests to their table places. No sooner than he did so, another man appeared at the doorway. He closed the door and sat next to the female guest. 'Welcome!' exclaimed Angus. The new group bowed their heads in unison.

'It has been too long since our last meeting,' said the last to arrive guest. His three companions nodded in agreement.

'Oh, I don't know if it's been too long,' smiled Anna, oozing sarcasm. She sat and swigged down the remainder of sherry in her glass.

An uncomfortable tenseness merged with the silence that followed the dry comment from

Anna. Simon broke the ice. 'We have much to discuss.'

'It's getting cold now,' said Sarah, rising to her feet. PJ agreed, 'Let's join the footy fans.' They turned to leave the frozen lakeside as the young lovers were passing, managing to avoid everything in their path while sucking each other's faces off. 'You've got to respect them, that is a definite talent,' added PJ. Seconds later they stood at the exit to the winter wonderland. He took Sarah by the arm. 'I can't work any of this out.' Not even her glowing smile could reassure him.

PJ pushed the door open and they re-entered the plain room. Julie looked a bit bored while Alex and Joe discussed Scotland's best ever football achievement.

'Don't tell me anything, Sarah promised to take me sometime,' demanded PJ.

'Great! I'll come with you,' said Joe.

Alex opened a door letting them back into the dining room. 'What game did you go and see?' asked Joe as they took their seats.

'Don't ask,' replied PJ.

An eerie silence seemed to mingle among the older guests. They smiled uncomfortably at each other as the youngsters sat down. PJ now sat at the middle of the large table with Sarah directly opposite. To his left was Joe then Alex, who were sitting across from Anna and Julie. Angus and Simon graced both ends of the table which also contained four new places.

The tall stranger sitting to the left of Sarah looked rather impatient as if feeling the need to say something but remaining quiet. He smiled in a tiresome manner while more than occasionally glancing over at PJ.

Sarah also seemed a little nervous, continually peeking at the new guests then down to Angus. She could sense the pleading in his expression. Sarah nodded before asking, 'Would you like more time to finish business before we eat?

'Splendid idea! I promise our discussions shall be concluded in an hour.'

The young group rose to their feet once again and headed for yet another door. After some eye contact and smiles from the strangers, they entered another white walled room. 'I know where we can get a quick snack,' said Alex already holding a doorknob.

'Oh no!' yelled Sarah as he pulled the door open. Wind and rain rushed into the room forcing everyone back against the wall. Alex let go of the handle, instantly disappearing into the storm outside. One by one the rest followed as wind hurled around the small room. PJ found himself running at an unnatural pace on a surface of sand or soil though nothing could be seen through the sheets of rain that battered them in constant waves. He decided to enjoy the ride while joining in with the faint human noises around him. 'Arghhh!'

Tension hadn't subsided in the dining room. Angus left the table to refill glasses leaving Anna and Simon smiling at the four guests. This group were known as the High Council. They were a panel of judges that assigned themselves to tasks that required judgement, always keeping a distance from the rest of the angelic community. The council consisted of Derek Spillat, Lawrence Pratt, Amelia Longthrift and leader Victor Swift.

Angus returned with drinks for everyone. Victor thanked him before taking a slow sip of brandy. He placed the glass down carefully and began. 'A simple R and T exercise has escalated into a breach in both our balance and time lapse.' His colleagues nodded in agreement, encouraging him to continue. 'We have spoken at length to Sarah and Alex advising them on the matter. PJ and Joe need to be returned to the original time and place, thus ending our difficult situation.'

'They refused,' said Derek Spillat.

'She refused,' added Miss Longthrift.

A few moments of silence followed. 'Sarah had her reasons. The fate contortion can be restored with minimal damage,' replied Simon.

Silence ate away at the already diminishing poor spirits. Eventually Victor lifted his brandy glass, not drinking just yet. 'I'm afraid a decision has been made.' He took another sip. 'Both boys shall be returned to one hour before the first time lapse, this I believe is when they are home alone preparing for a football match. The breach will then be closed.'

Victor leaned back casually on his chair and finished the brandy.

'And what of PJ?' asked Anna.

'Fate must run its course.'

'Fate is running its course.' Angus spoke in a voice full of anger and emotion.

'Not sufficiently enough and not according to our laws,' answered Victor.

'I would be grateful if you could enlighten us on these laws,' stated Simon.

PJ landed head first into what must have been a sandpit. Someone thudded against his back, and then two hands dragged him backwards into daylight. 'What a ride,' laughed Joe.

PJ agreed while spitting out sand. A world of white sand stretched in every direction to meet a dusky skyline and setting sun. An old wooden shack stood in front of them. A sign swung to and fro above the mesh door front, squeaking in the fresh evening breeze, The Sandpit.

'C'mon then, let's get a snack,' said Alex dusting himself down

'In there, look at the state of it,' remarked Joe. Dirty grey puffs of smoke rose up slowly from a rusty chimney jutting messily out of the timber log roof. The shack appeared to have seen better days. Dusty windows obscured any view of the interior. On approach it became apparent some maintenance of the panelled exterior was long overdue. Small leaves of peeling varnish flickered as if trying to free themselves and join forces with the passing wind.

'Remember everyone, we still have a meal to eat after this!' exclaimed Sarah as they entered. No one seemed aware of now being dry. It didn't matter once inside The Sandpit. Bacon frazzled eagerly next to other frying delights. The homely aroma penetrated welcoming nostrils. 'Stuff dinner! Two cheeseburgers please,' said Joe. A plump lady with red cheeks scribbled their orders down on a notepad. 'Coming right up! Our food doesn't ruin your appetite, so you won't need to stuff dinner young sir.' She winked at Joe.

'I love this place, make it three,' he replied. 'Same for me,' added PJ.

After an hour of grubbing out, the friendly lady retuned to the table. This time though she didn't carry a tray full of delicious food like her last four trips. 'Mr McEwen has asked me to inform you all that he is awaiting your presence at his home.'

'What happened to the full breakfast I ordered?' said Joe.

'I'm afraid you'll need to make do with the two you've already had,' she smiled.

'But I'm still starving.'

'I'll keep it warm till your next visit,' she promised.

The group headed for an exit sign above a door that previously had stated 'Toilets.' Sarah held PJ back as the others wandered through.

'No matter what is said when we go back, don't allow yourself to get angry. Keep your faith, promise.' Worry etched deep into her beautiful face.

'Keep my faith?'

'Yes, just stay cool.'

'Who are they?   Other people or angels? Have they got bad news for me?'

'Simon would never allow such a thing,' guaranteed Sarah. Her smile helped remove some of his doubt. Sarah continued, 'You are going to be a special man Master O'Hare.'

She pushed the door open. Angus stood in the small hallway. 'Welcome back.'

He held the door to the dining room open. Sarah found no comforting assurance in his forced smile.

Chapter 10

PJ sat opposite Sarah once again. During dinner she repeatedly tried to attract the attention of Angus only to find Victor Swift meet her every glance, which probably meant the tall dangly nuisance must have been happy with the outcome of their discussions. Simon chatted quietly to Angus as half-finished dessert bowls were pushed aside. Fresh coffee and a variety of biscuits and cakes hadn't even been touched when Angus slowly rose to his feet.

'Can I have your attention please?' The dining room fell into stark silence as he continued. 'You are all aware we have been joined by members of the High Council, who have kindly lent their worldly experience to helping our dilemma regarding PJ and Joe.'

Angus took great pleasure in adding that the Council were simply messengers from above. 'It has therefore been the decision of these wise knowledgeable beings to send PJ and Joe back to one hour before the first time lapse.'

'No!' shouted Sarah.

PJ laughed. 'What's the problem, we can always meet up again.'

'I'm afraid not,' answered Victor. He smiled smugly while adding 'On arrival to your destined time frame, all memory of the angelic world will be forgotten.'

PJ absorbed the info then decided he didn't like the outcome, letting everyone know with a frown.

'At least everybody won't think you're nuts being two hours late for a game,' said Joe trying to make light of the situation.

'Yeh,' replied PJ, concentrating more on Sarah who seemed really upset.

Victor rose to his feet. His colleagues quickly followed. 'Thank you for your warm as ever welcome.'

Angus tried to smile at Victor's comment but could only manage a grimace. Victor continued, 'On behalf of the High Council I would like to apologise to both young men for the upset due to the episode of errors. We bid you all farewell.' The Council members bowed and smartly exited using the same door in which they entered.

'Don't hurry back,' muttered Anna as the door closed.

'The departure of the High Council brought another uneasy silence. Everyone contemplated what the decision actually meant.

'This matter is concluded. Please refrain from discussing the issue.' Simon's words were firm and directed mostly towards Alex and Sarah. He offered his farewells before exiting through the same door as the Council members.

'Look at the time; it's after one in the morning. We better get going,' stated Joe.

'You don't need to worry about time dear,' replied Anna on her way back to the table with a sherry refill for Angus and herself.

'Once you go through that door, all of this will be forgotten,' added Angus, pointing to the far left of the dining room. He swigged over the sherry with his free hand.

'I don't want all this to be forgotten,' said Joe watching Julie make her way around the table to an already open door. 'I must get back,' she insisted. 'Until next time!' Julie heralded hope in her goodbye, turned and was gone. Joe stared at the closed door. A slamming thud echoed her departure.

Anna raised her glass. 'Such is life,' then polished off the sherry. She slid the empty glass over to Angus. 'If you don't mind dear.'

'Of course' He quickly returned with the bottle. 'No use wasting energy.'

PJ suddenly felt a touch of anger prey on his fear. 'Is there any point in asking what's next?' No one answered so he carried on. 'Ok, we go through the door and arrive back to normality, not remembering any of this or any of you.'

'That is their ruling,' answered Angus.

'Well why wait, let's go.' PJ dragged Joe to his feet as he walked past. Chairs slid back roughly on the wooden floor as the others got up to say their farewells.

Sarah approached PJ as he reached the open door. She took his hand.

'I suppose this is it then,' he said.

'Looks like it.' Teary eyes accompanied her defeated smile.

Anna had just kissed Joe on the forehead. Angus shook his hand while she turned to PJ and did the same to him. The touch of her lips caused a renewed calmness to spread through his worried mind. 'I'm sure we'll meet again,' whispered Anna, winking slyly.

'It's been a pleasure young man,' said Angus, following up his statement with a firm handshake. The boys stepped inside the doorway.

'Is there any chance of me bumping into Julie again?' asked Joe.

'Never say never.' smiled Angus. Sarah came forward and gave Joe a quick peck on the cheek before turning to PJ who got a slightly longer smacker on the kisser. 'Bye.' She stepped back to join Alex and Anna.

PJ and Joe felt so calm now, thanks to the help of Anna. It seemed as if they were about to head home after a good night out rather than embark on a journey through space and time.

'See you later guys,' said Alex as Angus closed the door.

'I'm starting to get fed up with these bright white walls,' said PJ, looking around the plain room waiting for something to happen. 'Me too!'

Mist gathered in the usual way, curling around their ankles and rising. It filled the small area quickly. 'Do you really think we'll forget all this?'

Joe didn't answer. He was already gone. PJ waved his arms around in the thick cloud trying to make contact. Bang! He followed Joe into oblivion.

The swirling mist thinned and cleared. In seconds it had returned to a clear bland room, empty and innocent of any happenings.

PJ stared dumbfounded at his football boots. After dropping them into the kitbag he gazed around the kitchen as if trying to remember something. Tyres churned up the driveway alerting him of Mum's arrival home. He crept out the back door and waited for her to go inside. As the front door closed PJ bolted out the gate and down Springfield Place. Sorry Mum but I can't get caught this time. He came to a halt at the end of the street, startled yet delighted by his realisation. PJ could remember everything.

Joe sat on the back seat of the minibus staring out the window as PJ bumped down next to him. 'Alright mate?'

'Well if you call knowing exactly what's going to happen in the next few weeks alright then I suppose I'm alright,' replied Joe.

Tam McGonnagle jumped briskly onto the minibus.

'Right, let's go!' His statement brought a wave of shouts and cheers. Old Jordy Fisher duly obliged, hammering the gear stick into first. A loud screech came from under the bonnet as the ageing vehicle set off.

'Anna must have done something to us with that forehead trick of hers,' said PJ.

'Well thought out Sherlock. I'm more worried about why she made us remember.'

They spent most of their journey to Thornton in deep silent thought. Bert Wallace and his big smug smiling face greeted the boys as they made their way into the away changing room. Tam smiled but you could tell he would much rather have given Bert a quick slap when walking past him. Thirty minutes later, Bridge East was stripped and ready for kick off. Tam went through his usual pre match talk. It always began with 'Right guys, here's the plan.' Joe noticed changes in Tams team talk.

'I thought everything had to return to its original happening,' he muttered.

'That's what they told us, why?'

'Things are changing already.'

Tam interrupted the boy's quiet conversation with a loud 'Excuse me! I suppose you two are concocting a far better plan for today's game.'

'We sure are boss.'

'Is that right Joe, you can tell me all about you're brilliant plans during the game cause you'll be standing at my side wearing a subs trackie.'

'Sorry Tam,' said Joe while lowering his head in embarrassment. Tam had to shout again to stop the outbursts of laughter. By the time he had finished, adrenalin was flowing in abundance. The boys exited the changing room like a mob fleeing a riot. Bert managed to keep his smug smile as the teams rushed into the warm sunshine.

Ten minutes after kick off, the smile had gone. It's replacement being five minutes of bemusement followed by another thirty of bewilderment. Bert was overheard saying how well wee Joe Watson reads the game. The second half went just as bad for Thornton. Poor goalie Billy Hunter looked positively scunnered as he retrieved the ball out of his net for the fifth time. Celebrations of PJ's goal drowned out the final whistle.

'Hard luck mate,' offered Tam, stretching out a consoling hand to Bert Wallace.

'Next time eh,' replied the gutted Thornton manager.

Over on the sideline stood Jack Watson and Andy O'Hare clapping as if their sons were about to lift the champions league trophy. The clump of bodies eventually dispersed from around PJ allowing him to get up. His heart sank when he noticed the four strangers dressed in long black clothes mingling among the home supporters. Victor Swift smiled at PJ before disappearing into the crowd. 'What's the matter mate, you look as if you've seen a ghost,' laughed Joe, rubbing PJ's head. 'Worse. It was those four dodgy characters from the High Council.

Andy and Jack made their way to the car park. 'Those two don't look too happy with the win,' said Andy, watching PJ and Joe enter the pavilion to get changed. The other boys were singing and laughing while they seemed to be in deep discussion about something.

'Maybe they're just being amicable in victory,' replied Jack

'Aye right, I think we'll need to keep an eye on those two.' The two dads laughed at the thought of their sons being amicable about anything.

PJ and Joe dressed quickly, trying to keep in touch with the celebrations while deciding on their next step. First of all, they would tell Tam their Dads would take them home. Then go out and tell both fathers that they were going back to Coalbridge in the minibus. This would give them a chance to think. 'Are you sure it was them?' asked Joe.

'It was definitely them,' replied PJ as they walked across the car park.

Old Jordy held a rag in one hand and the dipstick from his dilapidated engine in the other. He sighed at how thirsty for oil the heap of junk could get after a short trip to Thornton.

'Great result boys!'

'Brilliant,' agreed PJ.

'Have you seen four dodgy looking people dressed in black?' added Joe.

'Let me think. Is this a trick question or a joke about referees?'

'Naw, these people looked like they were going to a funeral,' said PJ.

Jordy thought for a moment while wiping his hands on the rag. 'Nope, but I bumped into Bert Wallace a minute ago. He looks as if he'd just been to a funeral.' Jordy gazed back down at the old engine. 'I think it's time for a new minibus boys.' His last comment went unheard. PJ and Joe were already out of the car park heading for the forest.

'Why don't we just go straight to Haystone Rd?' suggested Joe.

'No, that would mean we definitely remember. What if the Council were just checking up on us? I think we should go home as normal, get dinner and meet up in Brannigans tonight. If we bump into the gruesome foursome before then just pretend we don't know them. Hopefully Sarah and Alex will be there again tonight.'

'Does it really matter what the Council think? They're going to know something isn't right seeing as we're standing in this forest again,' replied Joe.

'Good point, stuff them. Let's go home.'

Sarah stared nervously over at Alex who returned her effort of a smile with caution as Simon shook his head for the tenth time. 'You could be in big trouble,' he said.

'I haven't done anything,' insisted Sarah.

Angus and Anna were sitting across the hallway, still discussing the harsh decision by the High Council. 'Jumped up messengers,' exclaimed Anna.

A door opened next to them. 'Could you please come in now,' said an elderly gentleman wearing red robes. Once inside, they sat on plain wooden chairs in front of a highly polished desk. Victor sat behind it smiling at them. Sarah checked out the decor in the office. She decided it was dull and boring like its occupier.

Victor cleared his throat in that same annoying manner. 'Ahem, I think we all know why you've had to be summoned at such short notice.'

'Yes so can we just get on with it,' replied Angus sternly.

'I have been instructed to cover every detail from start to finish. Let's have a brandy before proceeding,' said Victor.

'Great idea, make mine a double,' answered Angus.

PJ didn't enjoy mum's stovies quite as much this time round, feeling trapped under constant waves of déjà vu. The bizarre experience of having done this all before seriously affected his appetite. He found himself thinking that although going through motions for the second time, none of this felt as if it was really happening. Last time, Mum and Dad wore worried expressions because he had missed the game and was acting weird. This time, there was no mention of being late for work or any comments about the weird dream this morning, but it just didn't feel real.

'Not hungry son, after all that running around after a football?' said Mum sitting down next to him. He returned her warm smile.

'Not really, it must be all the excitement of gubbing Thornton today.' He pushed the almost untouched plate aside. 'I'll grab a snack later down at the club.'

Mum picked up the dinner plate as PJ banged upstairs in his usual manner. This time, last time or next time, it doesn't matter to a mother. She knew something disturbed her son

PJ dropped his mobile onto the bed after texting Joe. 'This is weird, I don't feel right.'

He headed into the shower. Hot water, soap suds, shampoo. Same night, same shower only a different set of problems. At least I know I'm not losing the plot. Silence and steam soaked into him as he pressed the off button. The rising steam made him feel uneasy. PJ grabbed the towel, stuck it around his waist and quickly left the bathroom.

Back in the bedroom James had begun his dressing preparations. 'Not again,' said PJ, a little too loudly. 'Eh?'

'Nothing, I hurt my foot on the door bar.'

'Which one?' asked James holding the two pathetic choices of shirts.

'The stripy one,' said PJ to see if his brother would opt for the same shirt.

'Nah, white with the pattern is the winner,' James stuck on the shirt while watching his reflexion in the mirror. 'A message came from Joe when you were in the shower,' he said.

PJ lifted the phone noticing it didn't display new message. 'Did you read my text?'

'Calm down, I only checked it to see if I needed to waste my time walking to the bathroom. Joe always sends you stupid unimportant messages.'

'What did he want?'

'Oh nothing in particular. Remember Dad going on about that mad woman from the eighties, Mystic Meg. She used to annoy everybody early in the morning on breakfast TV with her daft predictions of the future?'

'Aye.'

'Well, your mate says he feels like her,' commented James.

PJ placed the phone onto the bedside cabinet and proceeded to look for socks and boxer shorts while contemplating a relatively suitable answer. Eventually he laughed in one of those false pathetic laughs. 'That's because he predicted the correct score today. His dad says that sometimes. Who do you think you are, Mystic Meg?'

'Wow, get him to put a few lottery lines on for me,' said James checking the finished result from different angles in the mirror. 'Anyway, are you going to Brannigans? If so, don't cramp my style wee man. See you later.'

PJ finished dressing and sat alone in the bedroom. The silence troubled him. Would Sarah and Alex be at Brannigans this time? What made Victor Swift and his pals appear at the game today? Causing most discomfort though, why could he remember everything?

He suddenly became aware of breathlessness. 'What's going on?' he said out loud while panting for oxygen. Real fear took over. Tingling fingers prevented him reaching for his phone. Music blared out from downstairs. Dad was listening to The Smiths. PJ tried shouting out as his breathing turned to short staggered blips. Nothing could be heard amidst the turmoil building up inside his mind. He flopped backwards on his bed and stared unconsciously at the ceiling, a silent calmness settled his beating heart. PJ drifted off into the deepest sleep imaginable. He wouldn't be going to Brannigans tonight.

Chapter 11

A dusty old grandfather clock ticked loudly in the far corner of Victor Swift's office. It added annoyance to an already stirring atmosphere.

'We have been through the same details again and again,' insisted Simon.

'I appreciate all your assistance but my instructions are to make sure every aspect gets covered,' replied Victor.

'I told you he was no more than a message boy,' whispered Anna to Angus, just loud enough for Victor to hear.

'A simple exercise of R and T has caused quite a stir,' said Victor as he sat a silver tray of various drinks on his polished desk. 'Please, help yourselves.' He continued while pretending not to have heard Anna's harsh comment. 'This particular exercise was designed for our young searchers to reach into a person's mind and touch the senses, nothing more.'

'Sarah only acted on the overwhelming feeling that Master O'Hare had a future destiny involving saving thousands of lives, possibly more. It has been explained on several occasions,' said Anna. The other three members of the High Council had entered while she spoke and were now sitting opposite.

'Nice of you to join us,' mentioned Angus.

'Do I detect slight sarcasm in your words?' asked Derek Spillat.

'Indeed you do Derek and it's the first accurate detection you lot have managed since this matter began.'

'Well I never!' ranted an outraged Amelia Longthrift.

'Now you've got two in a row,' added Anna.

'Enough please,' insisted Simon, before continuing. 'The balance has indeed been breached and the time lapse altered. We are now dealing with a considerable fate contortion. In my opinion, your helping out in this situation has widened the breach.'

'What is the special interest you seem to have in the boy?' asked Anna before any of the Council members had a chance to reply to Simon's statement.

These comments would surely require a reaction from the Council. They became uneasy, looking at each other in an uncomfortable manner. Victor gazed at the paperwork in front of him as if seeking some clue overlooked. He fumbled with the pages, and then began.

'It has been the unanimous decision of the higher authorities that an undoing of the time lapse be carried out immediately.'

'Meaning what exactly?' said Angus.

'Without any interference this time.'

'Tell me you haven't terminated the boy's life?' pleaded Simon.

'You've killed PJ!' shouted Sarah.

'Excuse me young lady, but we had to enter the reality created for him by you. The boy was fully aware of our presence, which means a further enquiry and explanation will be required.'

'I did not create a false reality,' raged Sarah

Victor cleared his throat as a sign of continuing. 'PJ will return to one hour before the first time lapse, without memory, thus allowing his proper eventual happening to occur. This process is underway.'

'Murderers!' Sarah stormed out the room after her comment. Alex shook his head at the Council and followed her. Victor waited until the door banged closed before recommencing.

'A further meeting will be held into why the two boys were returned with memory.'

'Don't bother researching the matter. I did it, so leave Sarah Timmons alone,' said Anna pushing her chair back and heading for the door. Angus did likewise. Before closing it he turned to the Council. 'You have brewed a lasting storm this time.' Simon stood as Angus slammed the door shut.' I'm sorry matters are to end like this.' He bowed and left.

PJ blinked reluctantly as his eyes adjusted to the new surroundings, eventually springing open. He found himself staring wide eyed at an unearthly sky. Dark, ink blotted cloud raced across a blood red horizon. Dull shades of peaked mountain top merged with grey smoke in the far distance. Small dots appeared from within smoke. PJ slowly rose to his feet. He seemed to be trapped inside a gigantic crater-like pit. Concentrating on the dots that had gradually gotten bigger, he became nervous when noticing cloud swirling around slow flapping wings. They looked big for birds. By the time he realised it wasn't birds flying straight towards him, the creatures were almost overhead.

Alarm bells rang to the tune of self-preservation. PJ could find no cover in the barren landscape but decided running would be better than waiting. Each step crunched ash and brittle stone under foot. The dry, rotten surface tinged by the horrible red glow from above. A high-pitched screeching pierced his ears. He covered them with his hands as he ran. Whispers of, PJ, could still be heard though. If he wasn't in enough trouble, it got worse. The crisp, stony surface soon turned to thick ash, each step took him deeper and deeper until he stuck tight.

Struggling caused the ash clouds to increase in density around him. PJ coughed and spluttered black dust as the creatures landed behind.

He could feel the presence of the creatures at his back. A build-up of fear and anger gave him the strength to twist round and face his assailants. Large wings swept up and down instantly clearing the remaining dust, allowing PJ to set eyes on the dangerous group. A princely looking angel stepped forward. 'Greetings Paul Joseph, your arrival is late according to my calendar. I am David.' The tall angel bowed, shiny jet-black hair dropped and gathered in a mass almost covering his smiling face. He pulled the frightened boy up, freeing him from the ash pit.

'I am never going to fall asleep again,' replied PJ.

David and his five friends were dressed in dark brown, knee length leather like robes. Their long hair and rough appearances reminded PJ of gunslingers in Tombstone, only with wings.

'Do not be afraid.' David put an arm around PJ and lifted him off his feet. As they rose up through the crimson sky and over mountain tops, PJ knew two things for sure. Firstly, this didn't feel like one of his usual weird dreams. Secondly, deep down, nobody would waken him this time.

The Searchers returned to Haystone Rd. Angus offered Simon and Anna a sherry while they decided on the next sensible move. Every aspect had been contemplated. All roads led to the same destination. No matter which way they approached the problem, the outcome was unanimous. Something was not quite right with the High Council.

Sarah and Alex sat on a comfortable couch away from the elder group but close enough to overhear the harsh spoken words. 'May we be excused?' asked Sarah, jumping to her feet.

'Of course my dear, but I don't think it would be wise to contact PJ while he lies in limbo,' answered Anna, reading her thoughts.

'We just want to make sure he's ok,' said Alex following Sarah to the door. Simon stood and approached the youngsters. 'PJ will not have arrived in the normal fashion. Seek out David and ask him to put things on hold until further notice.'

Sarah nodded to Simon's instructions then she and Alex left through a door in the parlour taking them far from Haystone Rd. Simon closed the door on the young Searchers.

'I feel our High council is in a state of self-destruction,' he said to his two remaining colleagues.

'Good, let's help it along a little,' replied Anna. She sat her glass down, never losing her warm smile.

Alex followed Sarah along a long glass corridor. Mist refused visibility to the exterior but great warmth could be felt from beyond.

'It's been a while since we last took this journey,' exclaimed Alex.

'Yeh, David can be scary sometimes.'

'I wouldn't like to get on his bad side.'

David was ancient, even in angelic terms. Some reckoned among the first, though his early thirties appearance would suggest otherwise. Never having lived on earth, apart from a few required visits, he was of heaven's blood governed by heaven's hand. A creature of task designed to carry out heaven's will. David was a sort of death's doorway bouncer who met new arrivals and assisted them to their final destinations. Journeys had taken him from the far reaches of heaven to the very depths of hell. Over an abundance of centuries, the travels had added a rough edge to his handsome appearance.

Some new arrivals weren't too chuffed when discovering their final resting place. Let's face it; he's had a few dodgy customers over the years.

An expert in the field of his eternal vocation, methods were simple. Each new client would have their fate foretold to David before arrival. The motto of the workplace remained untouched throughout his long successful career. They go up through the gate or they don't.

PJ however, presented a rare problem to him, a welcome change to monotonous daily procedure, but nevertheless, a problem.

'What am I to do with you Master O'Hare?'

PJ didn't answer, he watched the comings and goings of countless winged angels as they carried out today's workload. David sat on a stone bench amidst his large chamber of cloud. PJ took a seat on a small stone stool opposite.

'Ah! Eighteen hundred and fifty seven.'

'Eh?' replied PJ, becoming more scared by the second.

'My last case similar to this.'

'Is that good or bad news for me?'

'A young boy supposed to arrive, didn't then did. It caused heaven and earth to rumble before resolving. This other boy also showed up as a discrepancy on my calendar.'

'Is that good or bad news for me?' asked PJ again. David didn't answer.

A burly angel entered through the wall of cloud. 'Two young guests wish to consult you about our new arrival.'

David stood quickly. His eyes narrowed and wings flicked up menacingly. 'Show them in.'

PJ watched on as the big angel disappeared momentarily then remerged behind two young angels. 'We bring a message from Simon.'

'Ah, I knew as much. Come sit, we have much to discuss.'

Sarah and Alex sat on the stone bench.

'Hi PJ,' said Alex casually.

'Alright?'

Sarah smiled at him. She looked even more beautiful in the light of this strange place. David paced around the chamber as if trying to work out a difficult puzzle. He turned eventually and addressed his new guests.

'Your parents are continuing their great work.'

'Busy as ever,' agreed Alex.

'Are you faring well?' asked Sarah politely. He shrugged his shoulders and sat between them. 'I tire sometimes. Centuries of witnessing our Lords simple rules of stone carved into cities of greed, breeding corruption and deception. They come to me, snivelling forgiveness thinking I can have any bearing on a fate self-created. The path you make is the path you take.'

Sarah and Alex lowered their heads, consuming his words. They had heard him speak of such things before, at the time of their own departure from normal human existence.

David joined them, head bowed in prayer. They held in their thoughts, hope for all those souls, good or bad. Without knowing why, PJ closed his eyes and prayed.

The three angels said a prayer for the redemption of lost souls while PJ chose his own words. Mum, Dad, James, Annie, anybody, please waken me up. David raised his head and waited until the others had done likewise before speaking. 'I was telling PJ how rare a situation we have here. You will both remember the date well.' David smiled and continued. 'Isn't it strange that I have the last such case sitting next to the current problem?'

PJ found the new silence irritating but not enough to question anybody so opted for quiet observation instead.

'The High Council is no doubt involved once again,' added David.

'Of course,' replied Alex

PJ caught a glimpse of David's wings flick up in frustration as the angel paced the floor again. Each feather, if indeed that, shimmered and shone while trapping then emitting wonderful colour. David turned to face the youngsters; his fascinating wings tucked themselves out of sight. 'Tell me Miss Simmons, what message has Simon for me?'

'He has asked that you put things on hold until further notice.'

'Fine, we shall do as Simon wishes.' David sat down between Sarah and Alex again. 'Tell me everything.'

After an hour of filling him in on all the details involving PJ and the High Council, Simon appeared through the cloud wall. David rose to his feet quickly and bowed. 'I have carried out your request old friend.'

'I am once again in your debt,' replied Simon bowing. He went on to explain that PJ must return to his first point of contact with Sarah and Alex. 'We shall mend any fate contortion and prevent the eventual happening which the Council deem to be his future destiny.'

'And what of my other supposed arrival?' asked David.

'Mr Fisher will not be making your acquaintance just yet.'

'Is that Jordy Fisher, what's wrong with him?' said PJ.

'Your friend is unharmed. Everything will be explained to you shortly,' replied Simon.

'Do you mean to send Master O'Hare back to first contact with full memory?' asked David, looking rather concerned.

'Yes, this is imperative.'

'Only a mere handful of humans walk the earth with heavens knowledge and consent,' commented David, becoming more interested

'PJ is to be one of them, at least for the time being.'

'Approved from above?'

'High above,' answered Simon who then turned to PJ and apologised for keeping him in the dark so long. 'We have been aware for some time of problems in our domain. So called friends seem to be making errors of judgement thus creating ripples of concern for others to smooth over while more important issues are overlooked. Names at this stage are irrelevant, more worrying is the fact that souls are being lost to the other side and a growing number of infiltrators work among us.'

'And so it begins again,' exclaimed David. He knew exactly what Simon was talking about, having returned souls to their rightful place on many occasions.

'God willing, you will agree to help us in our quest,' added Simon.

PJ stood up and paced the floor like David had done. The latest information gave him brain overload.

'Please allow us to stay with PJ until the time contortion has been mended,' pleaded Alex.

Simon put a hand on the shoulders of Sarah and Alex. 'You will both need to help your friend.'

Sarah looked worried. 'What about the walk of truth?' she asked.

'David will make sure no harm befalls him on his journey,' answered Simon. David smiled, as if looking forward to the task. PJ had been silent long enough. He sat back down and stared at the floor. 'Walk of truth, journey, can I not just open a door or get sucked into a picture?'

'This journey is a bit different,' laughed Alex, who continued. 'The walk of truth will allow you to see everything, almost.'

'I'm not sure I want to see everything, almost.' His half-hearted humour made the others smile. Simon sat beside him. 'On returning, all going as planned, your senses will be altered.'

'How do you mean?'

'It will be like acquiring a sixth sense.'

'I've seen that in films.'

'Not like this you haven't,' smirked Alex. Sarah nudged him. 'Try and be serious.'

'I'm just trying to keep PJ relaxed,' whispered Alex

'No one is ever ready for the walk of truth. Very few who thought they were, proved even more so that they weren't,' offered Simon.

'If that was meant to make me feel better it hasn't worked,' replied PJ.

'I have never lost a soul on a journey,' stated David with stark assurance.

'When do we go?' replied PJ. The thought of possibly upsetting David carried enough incentive not to ask any more useless questions.

Simon moved to the centre of the chamber and stared upwards. His distant eyes pierced the cloud ceiling. He broke free from the invisible grip after a few moments. 'We shall meet again soon.'

David nodded, with an excited smile.

'Same as last time boss,' smiled Alex.

Simon was well aware that Alex referred to his own walk of truth in eighteen hundred and fifty seven, resulting in shockwaves throughout heaven and hell.

PJ noticed a circle of the cloud roof above Simon begin to swirl and rise. When his eyes lowered he should have been astonished but wasn't. Simon had removed his jacket, revealing gold silk robes with matching coloured wings that flickered and fluttered, eager for flight.

'David shall guide you,' he promised. After a meaningful nod to the others, and a flick of his magnificent wings, Simon was gone. A circle of brilliant, blue sky drenched the room in light momentarily, and then the swirling cloud ceiling returned to normal.

'Time to go,' said David.

'Fasten your seatbelts,' added Alex.

David put his hands on PJ's shoulders. 'Remember this point of your life as when it changed forever.'

They left the cloud chamber amidst a rush of angry wind.

Little Annie wandered back upstairs in Springfield Place to take another peek into the bedroom, just to be sure of her former findings. PJ lay motionless. She stared at the sweating face of her brother. 'PJ are you drunk?'

His arms and legs began twitching as if by electric shock. Annie took a few steps back, not knowing whether to laugh or scream. 'Stop doing that or I'll shout on Dad.'

'David! Please help!' yelled the sleeping boy.

'That's it, I'm telling!' stated Annie.

PJ sprang to his feet before she got the chance to shout.

'Thanks, wow, what a ride.'

'Thanks for what?' asked Annie.

PJ felt a bit groggy. Everything seemed fuzzy for a couple of seconds while regaining some alertness. He was faced with an inquisitive little sister. 'What ride were you dreaming about and why did you say thanks, and who is David?'

PJ instantly lost the remaining colour from his face. He turned away from Annie, trying to recall the last minutes after departing the cloud chamber.

The eventual blip of memory nearly knocked him off his feet.

'I'm not supposed to be here!'

'Where are you supposed to be then?' said Annie, still standing behind. He swung around to tell her to beat it. His heart almost stopped when he realised what was in the room with them.

Chapter 12

PJ recognised the massive creature standing behind Annie, towering menacingly over the small girl. Unable to move or speak, he screamed her name but knew she couldn't hear him. He tried desperately to run towards her but was stuck tight.

The demon's wide eyes revealed pits of fire, burning deep into its meaty skull of a head that looked too small for the body. Pencil thin lips grimaced an echo of a smile. Horrible, blood red scales heaved to and fro on a muscled carcass as its breath of despair filled the room. The appearance of the demon looked like the result of a mad wizard taking a giant red fish and turning it into a weird, small-headed body builder, before setting its eyes on fire.

This was one of many who had halted PJ in his walk of truth. Their attack on the group had led David to catapult him to safety, thus PJ ending up back at the High Council's point of demise at home rather than first contact in Witchwood Forest.

Annie became frightened and confused by her brothers strange behaviour but was used to him playing practical jokes.

'Stop it! You're frightening me PJ.'

Still frozen to the spot, he reached far into his mind, searching for the strength to defend Annie against such a formidable monster. PJ found himself daring the beast to touch even the slightest hair on her head at its own destruction. He smiled while issuing the warning casually into the burning eyes of the beast.

'I mean her no harm Master O'Hare, if you will return with me,' hissed the creature into his mind.

PJ met the fiery stare as anger welled up, consuming all other thought.

'Dare!'

He felt his silent threat penetrate the very soul of the demon.

In a lightning flash, a dark silhouette appeared and grabbed the creature, dragging it down the hall until disappearing through the outside wall.

PJ was free from the invisible grip. His urge and momentum caused him to fall forward, landing face down at Annie's feet. Unharmed and unaware of the brief visitor, she turned and fled the room. 'Dad! PJ is drunk!' yelled Annie, banging downstairs.

Struggling for breath, PJ stumbled to his feet, disorientated and still angry. Something had entered his home, threatened his family. 'I'll find the thing and make it pay with its useless existence.' He spoke out loud while staggering towards the bathroom, only managing to close the door as Mum thumped upstairs.

'PJ are you alright, open this door now,' she demanded.

Breathing heavily, his eyes darted around the bathroom as if an answer lay within. At least the scale wearing, muscle bound red freak had disappeared.

'Mum! I'm ok.'

A shadow momentarily blocked evening sunlight from entering the frosted glass window causing him to back up against the door. Fish face obviously hadn't given up yet. Mum got more persistent. 'Open the door PJ!'

'In the name of God, let me deal with this.' His calm voice startled Mum. She stopped banging on the door as the shadow moved away, allowing sunlight to seep briskly inside the bathroom. Mum was just escalating into total fury about language and morals when the doorbell rang.

'Hi Joe, come in,' said Mr O'Hare opening the door.

'Alright Mr O, this is Sarah and Alex. We met them last week in Brannigans.' Joe knew too much info would probably get him into trouble so he made his way through to the lounge followed by his two new friends. Annie arrived behind the trio. 'Hiya Joe.'

'Hi sprout,' he replied.

'PJ's drunk!' she exclaimed quite bluntly.

'No he isn't,' said Mrs O'Hare removing Annie from the doorway and entering. 'Hello, I'm PJ's Mum. He had a bit of an upset stomach.'

Alex and Sarah introduced themselves while Mrs O'Hare disguised her worry with a trying smile. Sarah could sense this as she shook her hand. 'Are you from Thornton?'

'No, were staying with our aunt in Haystone Rd,' answered Sarah.

'Oh that's a lovely street. I don't think I've met your aunt.'

'Yeh they must be loaded,' added Joe trying to help change the subject.

PJ finished dressing and hurried back to the bathroom. After splashing cold water on his face he turned off the tap and stared at the small droplets roll down his solemn reflexion. It felt like a stranger gazing back at him. He wiped his face dry and quickly headed downstairs.

'Alright, ready to go?'

PJ only popped his head in the door to propose his wish that they leave instantly.

'Are you feeling better son?'

'Yeh Mum, I had a bit of a dodgy stomach but I'm fine now.' His acting was pretty impressive. 'We'll never get a snooker table at this rate,' he added, as the others joined him in the hall. 'Bye!' PJ snapped the front door shut.

Once outside, Sarah slipped a small stone like tablet in his hand. 'Swallow this.' PJ did what she asked without hesitation. He instantly became less confused and a bit clearer headed. 'What did I just take?'

'Something to dull the effects of the journey,' she explained as the group walked smartly out of Springfield Place.

'What went wrong?'

'It doesn't matter. Another plan is in place. We need to get to Haystone Rd. Prepare yourself, strange things may happen on the way.' Sarah spoke confidently.

Everything appeared normal during the first five minutes. Lawnmowers and hedge trimmers were going berserk as usual, cutting and carving masterpieces out of greenery. Then, as if someone pulled the plug on the world, they stood under a shroud of dark silence. A lamp - post flickered pale light above their heads. 'Oops, is this one of the strange things you were talking about?' asked Joe.

Alex huddled everyone together in the chilling darkness. 'They have found us,' declared the young angel.

David paid no heed to the swirling mass of cloud movement created by entry to his chamber. He was in an angry mood. Now standing before him was a battle hardened angel named Aster. If David resembled the modern day rock star then she epitomised the Goth version. Almost the same height as her boss, clear blue eyes narrowed slightly as she returned his smile. Jet-black hair slicked back into a ponytail that dangled over her left shoulder allowed full view of Aster's beautiful pale features.

'What news of Simon?' asked David.

'None yet, but I believe he is rather busy with the High Council.'

'Good, how are our young Searchers progressing?'

'Some of the Council enforcers have broken through.' Asters eyes seemed to sparkle with excitement as she delivered the grave news.

'Come my dear Aster, let's give them a warm welcome.'

The ceiling wisped and curled as David and Aster headed for present day earth.

Angus sat impatiently tapping along with the tick and tock of Anna's hanging clock which graced the window wall of her study. He held a glass of port in the other hand. Anna issued him with a, would you please stop that annoying noise glare, while topping up his drink.

'They should have arrived by now,' he said, checking the time.

'Patience dear.'

'How dare Victor Swift attack our group.'

A buzzer sound interrupted their conversation. 'It's the picture!' exclaimed Anna. They rushed out the study and up onto the mid landing where light emulated from a wall portrait. In the painting, David stood on a single rock which jutted out of an angry sea. A storm raged all around, blending sky with rising waves. His robes and long black hair swung behind in the facing wind while a glowing sun, high above, pierced the grey dullness below. Golden light poured onto David's fully expanded wings. Arms hanging in a meaningful manner gave the impression of an angel on a mission.

'Show off,' said Angus with a laugh.

They maintained eye contact with his piercing stare until mist suddenly engulfed the hall. It cleared quickly to reveal David standing before them, head bowed. Angus and Anna returned the gesture.

'Come quickly,' said Anna taking David by the arm.

She explained recent events while David seemed more interested in the dark burgundy glow on the table, cast by the crystal ceiling light on her bottle of port.

'The enforcers are to arrive in a few moments which means I have time to indulge in your hospitality,' replied David with a wink at Anna. She quickly poured a drink for her guest.

'Remember our week in the hills?' remarked Angus as he handed David the glass of port.

'My friend, it took me a century to get rid of the hangover,' answered David before swigging the drink down in one go. 'Not the way to enjoy port but I'm sure you'll forgive my ignorance under the circumstances,' he added, sitting the empty glass down.

'You're forgiven, now go please,' pleaded Anna.

David rose from the floor with a gentle flick of his wings. 'Prepare the journey. Aster is clearing the route ahead.' He turned transparent, bowed, and then shot through the wall. Silhouettes of his outline floated overhead for a few seconds before disappearing.

PJ grasped tightly between Alex and Sarah. She whispered in a strange language. Heavy breathing could be heard from Joe who was either mentally preparing himself for a great battle or just terrified.

'Are you alright mate?'

'You've got to be winding me up,' he answered.

If things weren't bad enough, the faint lamplight flickered out. The only escape from complete darkness was to look straight up where black night merged with lighter shades of moving cloud, offering some visibility but no relief. Straight ahead, high up in the dark sky appeared a small red dot. It became a ball of fire heading in their direction.

'They got through,' stated Alex. 'Stay close together.'

Sarah took PJ by the hand. 'You do believe?'

'Believe what?' replied PJ, more interested in the fast moving fireball coming at them.

'In our Lord?'

'Of course I do.'

'Me too,' ranted Joe, hoping for the darkness and the fiery ball to subside on his simple acceptance of God. Not to be.

The approaching firestorm brought with it a howling wind that threatened to lift the youngsters off their feet while a horrible wailing screeched overhead.

'Everyone kneel!'

Sarah had to scream her instructions to be heard. 'Let us pray.'

Alex started the prayer, everybody joined in.

'Our Father who art in heaven, hallowed be thy name,'

The young Searchers continued praying, holding on tightly to each other.

'Thy kingdom come, thy will be done on earth as it is in heaven,'

PJ opened his eyes and looked at the massive fireball. It had stopped about one hundred feet away and the same height up, pulsating as if in a building rage before exploding into thousands of fire bolts hurtling in all directions, then towards him. He broke free from the group and stood up, still praying. His three friends did the same. They held hands as the streaks of fire scorched a path across the dark sky.

'And deliver us from evil, Amen.'

Features became apparent within each approaching fireball. Wings formed as bodies etched free, scowling and spitting fire. The demons were close now.

'Is that swords they've got?' asked Joe.

Sarah and Alex stepped in front of PJ and Joe, shielding them. The boys quickly moved back alongside their new friends. 'Were in this together,' demanded Joe.

 Suddenly, sheets of white lightning darted from right and left, zapping the fiery creatures one by one. In seconds, only two flaming demons remained as the disappearing lightning returned the night sky to normal. 'Remind me to say the Our Father more often.'

Joe made his comment as the demons landed. Flames wisped and curled around their scale like bodies, then vanished within.

'One of those creatures came to my house tonight,' said PJ.

'They are Council enforcers,' stated Sarah.

'They're ugly Sons of a thousand haddock,' added Joe, obviously awaiting his nervous breakdown to occur at any time.

'Greetings,' said the gruesome twosome in unison.

'You have no right to be here,' said Sarah. The taller one on the left hissed. 'Miss Timmons, neither you nor your brother are in any position to question our judgement.'

'Be off!' shouted Alex. 'Aye beat it,' added Joe.

This request seemed to annoy the demon duo, who probably felt that no further conversation would be required with the foolish children. They took a step closer, concentrating on PJ.

'We mean you no harm,' the one on the right promised. PJ moved forward, feeling anger build up inside.

'What do you want from me?' he raged.

'Our master has instructed us to take you towards your destiny,' the smaller one added.

'Tell me, who is your master these days?' asked an assertive voice, from behind the searchers.

David stepped through the group, placing a hand on PJ's shoulder. He gently pushed him back in line with his friends. The creatures eased back slightly when recognising the voice. They bowed before the taller one spoke. 'What business brings you here David?'

'The safe journey of my friends.'

Enough had been said. The pathetic demons bowed, burst into flames then disappeared.
David turned around. It took a few moments for his smile to return.

'Not lost your touch with the enforcers,' said Alex. David laughed, 'Come, Anna and Angus await our presence.'

'We were just about to take those bad guys out,' remarked Joe, still trembling.

'I'm sure you would have made it so,' answered David.

'This is Joseph Watson,' said Alex.

'Greetings Joe.'

They began walking towards Haystone Rd. PJ noticed the appearance of David change instantly. Wings retracted as robes ruffled up to become a loose fitting shirt draped over blue jeans, finished off with trendy white trainers. Only then did he realise the darkness was gone. Saturday evening had returned along with sound of garden equipment and the smell of freshly cut grass. Joe hadn't noticed David change into a normal human due to the impact of everything else returning as it should be.

Anna sat her glass down in a hurry as the doorbell rang.

'Everything is in place, don't worry,' said Angus.

'I hope so,' replied Anna, rushing to the front door. She swung the door open expecting to be greeted by smiling young faces. On her doorstep instead, were the two enforcers who had just fled from David.

'We wish to discuss Master O'Hare,' said the tall one. Before Anna could reply, Angus barged past her. 'Leave, now!' Once again, the demons bowed then became scarce.

I recognise those two but can't remember their names,' said Anna.

'It's been a long time since they've had names,' replied Angus.

Anna followed Angus outside. David crunched his way up the driveway in front of Sarah and PJ. Joe and Alex casually strolled behind, in deep discussion over the recent scary events.

'How many times do I need to explain, in earth terms maybe ten minutes had past but in unearthly terms no more than a hundredth of a second had elapsed,' stated Alex as they strolled by Angus.

'Rubbish, somebody must have seen something,' replied Joe.

Angus followed the boys inside and closed the door. He locked it and joined the others who were now standing up on the mid landing. 'It's actually a lot less than one hundredth of a second that elapsed, so no one would have noticed anything,' he explained to Joe, who still seemed to doubt the whole scenario.

'We need to get to Angus's home,' said Anna, ushering everyone into position. No sooner had she spoke, than familiar golden mist appeared and covered them. When it cleared they were in yet another white hallway. Angus opened a door leading to his dining room.

'Please sit. We must discuss a few details,' motioned Anna.

A door on the wall behind her opened quickly. In walked Julie. 'What are you doing here? This situation is extremely dangerous my dear.'

'I want to help,' insisted Julie.

'We are glad to have your support,' said Angus pulling a chair out for her to sit next to Joe. Anna began talking but another door opened. Joe took the new time out to smile at Julie in that pathetic lovey dovey way. She smiled back causing his face to distort even more. He hadn't bothered looking in the direction of the new opened door until hearing PJ say, 'Wow!'

Joe turned to see what all the fuss was about. 'Wow!'

Aster stood before them. After bowing, she smiled 'I'm afraid this route is still rather busy.'

Joe leaned over to PJ. 'Do you get rock chick angels?'

'You must do,' replied PJ. Aster didn't help matters by giving the boys a somewhat wicked smile before continuing on a more serious note. 'It would be wise to take your other route.'

David stood immediately. 'Do as Aster says. I must go friends.' He wasn't smiling now. Someone or something would shortly face his wrath. They left through the same door.

'Ok boys she's gone, you can lift your chins up now,' said Sarah.

'What do you mean?' replied PJ on the defensive.

'Aster has that effect on most males,' laughed Julie.

Anna rushed behind Joe and flung open a door. 'Quickly, we must act now. Joe, you will travel back first. There is no time for further explanation. Fate must return to first contact.'

'We'll horsewhip Thornton again,' said Joe, entering the doorway

'No problem,' agreed PJ. Julie stepped forward and gave Joe a kiss on the cheek. He looked around at everyone, well chuffed, then a horrible thought occurred to him. 'Will I remember any of this?'

'Let destiny decide,' answered Angus, winking.

'Right then, see you all later, I hope.'

Anna closed the door then opened it again. Joe had gone.

'You next PJ,' she said, holding the door open. He slowly made his way around the table into the bright hallway. Sarah and Alex remained sitting. They seemed to be in deep discussion or simply ignoring the departure of their new friend.

'They look awful upset to see me go,' muttered PJ to Anna.

'Don't worry, they are finalising important plans. Sarah and Alex will be joining you in your true reality. We will all be at your side if required.'

'Oh right, I thought I was getting the old brush off.' He smiled and then paused for a second as his face returned to an expression of doom and gloom.

'Things are going to be fine eh?'

His voice carried the pleading of a boy who had never needed to feel such insecurity or uncertainty.

Anna hugged him tightly.' Of course it will, just wait and see.'

'Life shall be as it should be,' added Angus, patting the frightened boy gently on the back.

As Anna closed the door, PJ caught a last glimpse of Sarah. Her smile assured him that everything would be fine, if such a thing was at all, even half possible.

'More blooming white walls.'

Chapter 13

It wasn't until Anna closed the door that PJ noticed how small the area had become. More in fact like a white walled cubicle. He braced himself while waiting on the usual mist to arrive.

I feel as if I'm stuck inside a fridge with no shelves. But then if I was, it would be dark. Who cares, where's the cloud? A small green dot appeared on the wall, entrancing him as it grew. PJ tried to focus but found it hard to keep his eyes open, then. Bang!

Grassy landscape replaced the white wall, hurtling towards him at an alarming rate. The harsh accompanying wind was too much. He closed his eyes. PJ was trapped inside a deafening whirlwind. Cool air suddenly replaced the blowing gale. He opened his eyes to Witchwood Forest. It wasn't hurtling towards him anymore. He was travelling through it, really fast. 'Arghhh!'

PJ cascaded down the winding slope towards the tar mac lane to Thornton, instantly pulling the brakes knowing that Mrs Muir would be at the bottom with her wee dog. He bumped onto the lane smoothly and came to a halt.

No sign of the old lady or her dog. A check up and down the lane verified his worry. Sight, sound and smell were all quite accurately familiar but no Mrs Muir or Mr Milne. He cycled along to the point of first contact. This is where he encountered Mr Milne and the talking bush, later to be known as Sarah and Alex. So much had happened since that particular Saturday afternoon. PJ paused for a moment recalling the various conversations with Frankie and especially the bush. Then there was that strange mist enveloping him, making things happen, again and again. How scary the last journey here had been. Everything felt clearer now but if this was the true reality, where were Mrs Muir and Mr Milne?

A flicker of shadow from deep within the dense tree line caught PJ's eye. The dark shapeless form moved towards him. Trip down memory lane over, time to go. Pedalling frantically, he knew the following shadow easily matched his step up in pace. It brushed and glided through the greenery like a hunter goading its prey before pouncing. Menace attached itself to the mysterious black shape as it moved out the trees over his head. It cast a familiar shadow on the ground. Either a giant bird had come to Coalbridge looking to steal a bike or he was being perused by an angry dark angel. A quick glance above, ended speculation.

'Arghhh' Why couldn't it have been the flying bike thief.

The horrible creature whispered, 'Pee… Jay…,' in such an irritating tone that P.J. wanted to stop, get off the bike and slap it senseless. If only it wasn't so terrifying. PJ opted for staring straight ahead while trying to shut out the murmuring breath tingling the back of his neck. Two figures stood ahead at the end of the forest lane. Sunlight glistened off the welcome to Thornton sign, preventing him from identifying who it was. Through the mirage type glare were two dark silhouettes, hands on hips while watching his approach. With eagle man above, tearing at his soul with its piercing tone, PJ could only hope the two figures up ahead were Batman and Robin.

Old Jordy watched on as the last boy exited the minibus joining his team mates in a chorus of 'Bridge East, Bridge East' while heading into the away changing rooms. He would nip over to Forestfield service station before the game to check the oil and tyre pressure. Jordy was tired of the constant maintenance required to keep the squeaking rust bucket road worthy. After carrying out the usual escapade of getting into the driving seat and getting comfortable, he finally turned the key sparking the unwilling engine into life. A chap on the window startled him. 'Blooming heck!' Jordy turned to meet the smiling young teenager.

'Is your ford a 94?' asked Alex, once the window had squealed down.

'It's actually a 93 son.'

'They built them to last back then. Any chance of a wee look under the bonnet?'

Jordy snapped back the bonnet lever, suddenly taking a bit of renewed interest in his once prized possession. 'Do you like old engines son? I suppose five minutes won't make a difference.'

'Let's hope it makes a world of difference,' whispered Alex to Julie as the old fellow made his way around to lift the bonnet.

Sarah tapped nervously on a small electric box at the forest entrance. Angus and Aster stood on the lane, hands on hips as PJ approached with his unwanted company.

'This will be an absolute pleasure,' said Aster, before sprinting towards them as the winged beast lifted PJ and his bike off the ground.

PJ closed his eyes. He felt the demon grip burn into his shoulders before releasing him.

'Hi PJ!' His eyes sprang open to the smiling face of Aster. They were floating in a grey void. 'What happened to the thing that lifted me up?'

'It had to leave in a hurry.'

'Where are we going?'

Aster placed a finger over his pleading lips. 'Get ready for a rough landing. Remember to keep your eyes open.' She smiled then disappeared. PJ didn't get a chance to ask any more questions before a bolt of lightning cracked across the grey horizon. Up ahead, bright light unzipped the greyness into blue sky. It was the sky above Witchwood Forest to be exact. PJ held on tight as he began the journey down to the narrow lane below. 'Arghhh'

Jack Watson watched from behind his checkouts, making sure everything flowed as it should. He occasionally enquired. 'How is Duncan getting on Sadie? Did you find the barbeque sauce Mrs Jones?' Jack paced the along, checking up each aisle. 'Need a hand madam?' His number two in command, John Logue was assisting Mrs Mitchell over at tinned soups. A stronger than usual urge to forget priorities made Jack glance at his watch. The game against Thornton would kick off in thirty minutes. Why not, I'm the boss. He issued John with a few instructions before heading through the sliding doors. Jack loosened his tie and pulled it off in similar fashion to Joe and PJ earlier in the day. He took a deep breath of fresh air as he threw the tie and jacket casually onto the back seat of his car. Jack was looking forward to taking his mind off things for a while. 'C'mon Bridge East'

Joe sat in the changing room fumbling with his boots. Something was wrong. He had a weird sick feeling like waiting for something bad to happen.

'Have you gone deaf son?' yelled Tam McGonnagle, bringing him out of his trance.

'Sorry Tam, I was dreaming there.'

'No kidding. Anyway, where is he?

'Who?'

'Who do you think, your mate PJ. I can't get him on his phone.'

'Erh, I'll nip out and see if I can get a hold of him.'

'Hurry up son we've got a game to win,' added Tam trying to instil some urgency into the boy. 'No probs!' replied Joe wandering out the room. The car park was busy. Cars were stopping here and there dropping off young excited players as teams gathered. Parents chatted among themselves, trying to avoid the odd flying ball heading their way. It doesn't matter where they are or what direction it goes, when some kids see a football they need to thump it anywhere.

Joe noticed Jordy over at his minibus, bonnet up. A boy and girl stood beside the old guy as he pointed at various parts of the engine. Joe approached them. 'Have you broken down mate?'

'Naw son, these two young people are interested in my 93 engine.'

'Why? It's a heap of junk, I thought you hated the old rust bucket?' replied Joe, much to the amusement of the strangers. The boy stepped forward, introducing himself and his friend.

'Alright, I'm Alex and this is Julie.'

'Alright, have we met before?'

'Not in this lifetime mate,' answered the boy. Joe found it hard to stop staring at the dark haired girl. Not only was she beautiful but also smiling at him in a more than friendly manner.

'Why are you not in getting changed?' said Jordy.

'Tam sent me out to look for PJ, have you seen him around?'

'I'm sure your friend will be on time for the game,' said the strange, gorgeous girl.

'Yeh,' Joe agreed without realising he had did so.

Alex and Julie quickly turned their heads up to the forest entrance. Without another word, they ran off.

'What was all that about?' commented Jordy.

'I don't know mate but something's not right,' remarked Joe as they watched the strangers sprint across the car park towards the forest.

Sarah and Angus waited, faces drenched in worry. It had been ten seconds since PJ had disappeared. Angus led her behind the large stone pillars at the forest entrance. 'I think it will be safer to stand here for a moment or two,' he said through a nervous smile. No sooner had they positioned themselves behind the lumps of stone, PJ appeared.

'Arghhh!' then 'Wow!' as he hit the ground, swerving and swaying to keep balance. The bike sped past them, straight across Thorntonhill Rd into a picnic area narrowly missing the wooden tables and chairs.

'That's PJ up there, what's happening?' Joe pointed at picnic area.

'What's he playing at?' replied Jordy. Joe was already running towards the erratic cyclist. A greyish coloured cloud seemed to follow PJ as he swung in and out of benches and people before managing to steer back onto the road.

Sarah could feel that same sick sense as last time but was unable to intervene. Destiny had to run its course in order to put an end to the ever-occurring cycle.

PJ on the other hand was more interested in the cycle causing him to speed down Thorntonhill Rd uncontrollably. He pulled at the brake lever which had no effect. If anything, he was speeding up.

Joe jumped the fence half way up the hill where Alex and Julie stood. Alex grabbed his arm as he landed. 'Stay here Joe, don't get involved,' pleaded the young angel. Joe looked at the stranger then up at the other two at the top of Thorntonhill Rd. PJ was now half way between them. 'Who are you people? Who are they?' shouted Joe pointing up at Sarah and Angus. He struggled free and pushed Alex to the ground. Julie stepped between them. 'You must not stop his journey,' She took his hand before adding 'Please trust us.'

Joe hadn't noticed everything come to a halt while Julie spoke but her comforting assurance calmed him. He looked down at her hand in his then back up to her smiling face.

Jordy decided to investigate. It wasn't like Joe to bully a smaller boy. Good as his eyesight may be, he couldn't quite make out what was happening further up the hill. Jordy walked smartly across the car park towards the foot of Thorntonhill road to get a better look.

Aster appeared beside Angus and Sarah as PJ continued his unstoppable journey. It looked like a faint swarm of bees clouded around his head and shoulders.

'They are still with him. We need to act now,' said Sarah in a frantic voice.

'Not yet, it will only allow more time to interfere with the eventual happening,' replied Angus.

'Patience child! This path shall run its course,' smiled Aster.

'Are you sure we've not met before?' asked Joe, still holding the girls hand.

'Why, do you think you have?'

'I'm not sure.'

Julie gently let go of his hand, bringing reality back to Joe.

'Arghhh!' PJ sped past.

'Slow down!' yelled Joe sprinting after him.

Thorntonhill Rd sloped down the forest edge where it merged with Parkside St, which ran along the bottom perimeter of Witchwood. The roads met at a mini roundabout put in place to reduce the speed of traffic due to the thick corner of trees causing poor visibility in both directions. Nobody had a better view of unfolding events than Jordy Fisher. He moved slowly towards the junction but his mind razor sharp, knew that the boy was going too fast and faced danger if any vehicle came along Parkside St. Jordy burst into a run when the large black car roared around the bend towards the roundabout.

Jack Watson pressed disc number three of Classic Hits of the Eighties. He sang along to 'Don't you want me baby,' while turning into Parkside St. Jack tapped the steering wheel in beat to the music. It brought back fond memories of a time gone by, new experiences, bad haircuts, weird dancing and more bad haircuts. He laughed at the very thought of his once proudly worn mullet. 'You were working as a waitress in a cocktail bar!' Jack belted out the words unaware of his increasing speed or the dark presence attached to his soul.

A cold surge of intense precaution washed over Sarah. 'Another force is now at work,' she warned.

Angus removed his tartan collared tweed jacket and handed it to her. 'Well spotted my dear. You are becoming quite an accomplished Searcher.' He smiled before turning to Aster.

'Let's put an end to these matters.' The smile vanished with his words, leaving only cool, calm intent.

'With pleasure,' answered Aster in obedience.

Sarah began running alongside Aster and Angus but could only watch on as they suddenly shot ahead. She caught a glimpse of a young, agile Angus leading the way for his female companion before they both vanished.

Further down, Joe, still in hopeless pursuit of PJ felt a whiplash of wind rush past. He tried desperately to keep his balance in its wake but stumbled left and right then head first onto the hard unforgiving ground. Elbow, head, shoulder, body. This was the sequence of pain issued to Joe from his brain letting him know it would shortly be going into shut down mode for a while in order to deal with these unwanted sensations. He stared up at the sky until his eyes closed, allowing a much needed nap. In his dream a beautiful girl leaned over him. Her long hair tickled as she lowered and kissed his lips. It was the girl he just met a few minutes ago.

Why did she kiss me? Who cares? The girl smiled as her outstretched hands helped him to his feet. Joe wanted to stay in this slow motion, comforting world forever. He could dance within the sparkle of her dark brown eyes

Slap! 'Snap out of it!' Stark reality returned, courtesy of Julie's hand. She grabbed him by the arm and began running after Alex and Sarah. He didn't even notice the aches and pains from the fall subside while observing the bizarre scene in front of him.

PJ had almost reached the bottom of the hill. A boy and girl were close behind. Old Jordy waved his arms in the air, running flat out towards the mini roundabout. Joe sped past his new friend. 'Slow down mate!' he shouted, breaking free from Julie.

Jack Watson got a startle when his compact disc player snapped off, bringing an eerie silence to the interior of his car. He was going too fast to stop at the junction. God willing, nothing would be coming down Thorntonhill Rd. Banging the brake pedal to the floor, Jack held his breath in fear as the tyres screeched towards the blind junction. His heart froze when he saw the old man waving at him from across the junction.

Quick as a flash of thought, horrifying events unfolded. Joe stopped running. The girl caught up and put her arm around his trembling body. Joe let his mind carry him to a world of surrealism where things could be viewed in a fiction-like fashion but not necessarily believed. The boy and girl who were running in front had suddenly disappeared just before the black car made crunching contact with PJ.

Joe allowed himself to slowly walk forward through his world of unreality.

The twisted bike frame folded under the large bonnet as if being consumed by an angry beast, while his best friend thundered against, then over the halting vehicle.

Even in this conscious realm of self-inflicted fiction, Joe couldn't stop the build-up and overflow of tears as he helplessly watched the contorted body of PJ hurtle through the air.

Joe dropped down onto his knees and stared at small tears splashing dark, wet marks onto the road. He wanted to get up and run towards his mate but daren't. Instead, he chose to delve into the safety of his imagination where PJ remained unharmed. A hand of comfort came to rest on his shoulder.

Jack Watson's short journey from his supermarket to Thornton would be one of weird recollection. Guilt from leaving John with added responsibilities had simply diffused into self-indulgence of his own needs. On impact with the bike however, Jack wished he'd stayed at work. He caught a glimpse of the boy who cracked the windscreen before vanishing over the roof of his BMW.

Jack recognised PJ while his own body jolted forward, face thudding against the exploding air bag. As his head bounced backwards to meet the headrest, he drifted into shock, unable to move.

Jordy Fisher approached the car. Wrenching pain increased in his chest as he viewed the sickening scene. An angry engine hummed its wrath, pinning the mangled bike frame underneath. Panic had ceased, leaving only outrage. He banged the window at Jack. 'What were you thinking man?'

Jack didn't answer. He stared at the blankness of the inflated airbag.

Jordy had almost reached the boy when an excruciating pain clamped around his overworked heart. He could walk no further. A watery substance rippled around the still body of PJ. It was the last thing Jordy saw before his blurry eyes turned everything to darkness. He fell limply onto the grass before getting a chance to help his young friend.

Chapter 14

Joe felt a warm rush of relief flow through his grief stricken body. He looked up to meet the friendly eyes of an elderly lady. 'What did you just do to me?'

Puzzlement secured a place within his new found relaxation.

The lady smiled while helping him to his feet. 'A little reassurance.'

'Thanks.'

Her outstretched hand met his. 'My name is Anna Cooke and I need you to trust me.'

'I'm Joe Watson. I trust you but we've got a bit of a situation ongoing here.' Joe never took his eyes from the crash scene as he explained

'You see, that's my Dad down there in his car. He's knocked my friend about twenty feet into the air, landing in a heap. The old guy lying next to him is our team bus driver. So without sounding rude Anna, I fear the worst right now.'

Anna led him down the road.

'Everything will be fine, you'll see.'

Thornton playing fields continued its usual hustle bustle as if nothing had happened. The incident seemed to go unnoticed to the world around them.

PJ once again sat in the familiar surroundings of the chamber of cloud, trying to remove all negative thought from his mind. Alone in this mysterious room of swirling mist he contemplated feelings of the last journey here which apparently signalled an ending to human existence as he knew it. Where was David this time? Surely I can't have died twice, thought PJ. Deep inside though, burned an overwhelming relief that this particular journey had indeed excused him from an appointment with some serious pain.

Jordy Fisher suddenly appeared through the cloud wall looking like he'd just received a left hook from Mike Tyson. He swaggered around in a trance for a few moments before noticing PJ.

'Thank God you're alright son,' he said, grabbing the boy by the arms.

'I think you better sit down mate.'

Only then did Jordy take note of the surroundings. He slumped down next to PJ and became transfixed by the moving walls and ceiling.

'Everything is going to be fine,' added PJ trying to ease the confusion.

'I saw you getting knocked into the air by a car,' replied Jordy, eventually.

'What else can you remember?'

'Pain, then sleep.'

'I think you had a heart attack.'

'Do you think so,' laughed Jordy. 'I think we've had more than a heart attack. We're up in the blooming clouds son.'

PJ couldn't help himself. He joined Jordy in a fit of laughter which came to an abrupt halt as a serious looking figure entered through the wall of cloud. Jordy stood immediately.

'Are you Gabriel?'

'No, I am Simon.'

'Alright?' added a slightly hesitant PJ, before turning to Jordy. 'Gabriel?'

Jordy shrugged his shoulders. 'It could have been'

'Please do not be alarmed Mr Fisher. This experience will be no more than a faded dream when you awake.'

'I feel pretty much awake now Simon.'

'I'm afraid PJ needed some assistance and our only option was to bring you both here temporarily while matters were being dealt with down below.'

'So were not dead then?' enquired Jordy.

'You're both very much alive.'

'Hear that pal, were not dead.' A much relieved Jordy rubbed PJ's head.

'Brilliant,' smiled PJ fixing his hair.

'Please accept our deepest apologies for having to intervene in such a manner but we had to put you both somewhere safe until being sure there would be no other attempts at meddling with your fates.'

'When can we go back?' asked Jordy.

'Can you feel a slight tightness around your heart?'

Jordy put a hand to his chest. 'Now that you mention it, I do feel something not right in there.'

'Don't worry, your body is telling you it's now time to return to normality. Simply close your eyes and wish it so.'

Jordy followed Simon's instructions only briefly before his eyes sprang open. He looked at PJ. 'Why are your eyes not closed?'

'I don't think I'm supposed to go back yet.'

Jordy cast a suspicious glare at Simon. 'You wouldn't be trying to pull the wool over my eyes to get rid of me then keep the kid here by any chance?'

'I promise you,' answered Simon 'His face will be the first you see when you awake.'

These words were enough to diminish any mistrust from the doubting old codger. He nodded to Simon who smiled while returning the gesture.

'See you soon pal.'

'Sure will,' replied PJ.

Jordy felt tired now. He allowed his eyes to close freely this time, hoping that the invited sleep could remove the fastening belt like grip around his aching chest. PJ watched on, horrified as the old man clutched at his shirt hopelessly trying to ease the tightening sensation before disappearing. Swirling cloud replaced the vision of Jordy Fisher.

Simon sat next to PJ. He noticed worry cast itself like a gloomy rain cloud over the face of the boy. 'Your friend is a great man. He will not waken until you return. Let's chat a bit. The rest will do you good before kick off against Thornton.'

PJ had forgotten his intended destination. The reminder perked him up to unimaginable heights. 'That's right, the game!' he stated with new found enthusiasm.

A soft smile covered Simon's serious expression as he began, 'Your walk of truth, though interrupted must be allowed to conclude. Against our hopes, we were sure that further attempts would be made by the Council to interfere. They continue to arrogantly refuse to accept what is to be and the different scenarios that need to be in place. One of which, is the path you now take'

PJ nodded in agreement without fully understanding what he had just agreed to.

'What do you recall from your journey before David had to intervene?' asked Simon.

PJ thought about the strange brief encounter for a few moments before answering

'Not much really. I remember being really happy then sad.'

'You were beginning to witness the highs and lows of mankind.'

'I didn't think much of the lows then,' replied PJ with a nervous smile.

Simon used the relaxed silence that followed to ease gently into a more pressing issue.

'How did you feel about the Council enforcer entering your home?'

A vivid memory of the incident accompanied Simon's question. PJ didn't answer at first. His mind flooded with rushing streams of anger that drowned any other thought or concern.

'How dare that thing come to my home.'

'You wanted to hurt the beast?'

'I wanted to do more than hurt it,' PJ's words carried venom. Simon seemed to understand. 'The journey can have a strange effect on senses,' he said.

'Thanks for getting rid of it.'

'We didn't, you completed that task yourself,' added Simon.

PJ felt a bit ashamed by his aggressive antics but proud of dealing with the demon on his own, even if he still wasn't quite sure what he had done to cause the beast to flee. Simon didn't give him much time to dwell on his shortcomings. 'I think it's time to put your friends out of their misery.'

PJ agreed. 'How do I get back?'

'In the same manner as Mr Fisher.'

PJ closed his eyes. Before truly wishing to return, he reopened them and took a quick glance around the swirling cloud chamber, then to Simon. 'Do you think it ever rains in here?' he joked.

'Go,' instructed Simon.

Within seconds, PJ had departed leaving Simon alone amidst the moving mist. He smiled to himself while shaking his head.

Joe reached the bottom of Thorntonhill Rd keeping a tight grip of the strange woman's hand. He used his free arm to wipe the stinging tears blurring his vision towards the crash scene. A blonde haired girl knelt beside the lifeless body of PJ. Another girl stood over them. It was the one who had kissed and slapped him. She smiled his way. Joe had definitely met her before. A ticking hum came from the car directly in front of him. He could only look at his Dad momentarily. Jack Watson's pain instantly transferred to his son, etching a scar of self- guilt that threatened to overcome the boy. Over on the right, lay Jordy Fisher in a crumpled heap. A young lady and an elderly man were walking smartly over to the poor old fellow.

Joe wished again that he could return to the safety of his inner imagination where such horrific things as these were not possible, but another build-up of tears, brought with their escape down his face, a stark, cold reminder of reality, a horrible, unavoidable truth that ate stealthily at his disbelief. Joe joined his Dad in a state of shock. Anna, aware of this, led him over to where PJ lay and allowed him to stare aimlessly along Parkside St. Angus joined the group. Together with Sarah and Julie they formed a circle around PJ. Anna gently let go of Joe who continued his empty stare just outside the newly formed ring. She took the outstretched hands of Sarah and Angus. Once the circle was complete, they closed their eyes.

Instantly, a shapeless haze rippled around the outline of PJ. Transparent waves became glints of pale colour as sunlight merged with the watery substance, slowly pulling free from the motionless body. It rose up to head height like a quivering see through jelly.

Sarah and Julie let go of their grip on each other and edged slightly apart, leaving a vacant space, which the wobbling shimmer floated into. It changed shape while filling the gap. Within seconds it resembled a waterfall in the contours of a human form.

Joe remained oblivious to the eerie silence and also the spectacular burst of colour that exploded on the arrival of David. 'Greetings, everything is in place', said the smiling angel, joining hands with Sarah and Julie.

'Time to bring him home,' stated Anna.

They lowered their heads, eyes firmly focused on PJ, willing his soul to return to the lifeless body. Return it did, with a vengeance.

PJ heaved and twitched as if being electrocuted then resumed a peaceful stillness. His chest gently raised and lowered while air introduced itself to starved lungs. Eyes opened slowly, blinking at the bright sky above. He jumped to his feet like a dazed wounded animal scanning the concerned faces around him with hateful contempt then bewilderment set in.

'Welcome home,' said Anna. PJ flicked his head towards the voice but didn't answer.

'You're safe now,' added Sarah. Again he turned to meet the new sound while staying silent. On eye contact, Sarah felt herself reach into the distant stare. Amidst the burning fury somewhere deep inside his pain, she whispered, 'Come home.'

PJ dropped to his knees gasping for breath. After about twenty seconds he sprang to his feet. 'Wow, what a ride!'

Angus rushed forward and grabbed him by the arms. 'What do you remember?'

PJ never lost his smile while answering. 'I think I've just completed another bit of my walk of truth' The group breathed a massive sigh of relief. Anna turned to Joe who still seemed oblivious to all around him. She kissed his forehead and waited, hoping the boy could exit the trance with no recollection of the horrifying events. Anna knew that Joe would carry a mental scar for a while, without actually knowing why he felt the upset. PJ moved in front of him as he came round. 'Alright mate? I thought you were a goner,' said Joe.

'Aye, close call,' replied PJ casually, before turning and taking the few steps to where old Jordy lay.

Jack Watson got out of his car. A look of disbelief had replaced the face of shock. He explained for the second time to the young inquisitive boy Alex, the driver's airbag had inflated. 'Look, its fine,' replied Alex, while Julie pushed the undamaged bike. Jack observed the bike then the unhurt PJ before allowing relief enter his brain. He gazed over at Jordy Fisher, unaware of the elderly lady touching his forehead.

Jordy lay as if in a comfortable sleep, head nestled on the lap of Aster who carefully stroked his forehead. PJ knelt down beside them. As he did, the old guy slowly opened his eyes.

'Alright mate?' smiled PJ.

'I thought you were in trouble son, I must have fallen.' said Jordy. He let his head tilt slightly until he found the smiling face of Aster.

'You've suffered a slight heart attack brought on by over exertion and stress.'

'But I'm as fit as a fiddle hen. Are you a doctor?'

'Yeh, sort of,' answered Aster, helping Jordy to his feet. They strolled off in the direction of the playing fields. The others followed on behind. Joe appeared to be overcoming the state of shock due to undivided attention from his beautiful new companion.

'What did you say your name was?' he asked.

'Julie.'

'Are you sure we've not met before?'

'Not in this lifetime anyway,' she smiled.

'Fancy watching a game of football?'

'I love football,' she insisted.

Joe couldn't believe his luck, a babe that loves football and possibly likes him. He strutted alongside the ten out of ten explaining how important this particular fixture was to Bridge East.

Angus and Anna observed the scene from behind. Matters, for now, were resolved. David stepped alongside them, content that his own task had been completed.

'Thank you for your valuable help,' said Angus.

'It is an honour and a pleasure to be of assistance.'

They watched on as Jack Watson drove off. PJ pushed his bike with one hand, the other was busy waving around, helping him describe recent events to Sarah and Alex.

'I foresee more adventure in the near future involving this young man,' stated David.

'So do we,' laughed Anna.

Corruptible souls would blend innocently among the strong of heart in their futile attempt at being overlooked, but the honest prying eye would begin the task of seeking out those responsible. Sooner or later they shall be exposed. Evil cannot lie dormant for too long. The impulsive need to destroy anything appearing to be good causes an urge to invite itself at the first opportunity. Time though, will bring them to the surface eventually, like the worm to a rainy day.

The Searchers intended using this quiet period for reflection and thought, while more importantly, keeping a watchful eye on PJ and Joe. They were after all, embarking on July 5th for the third time. Hopefully, there would be no need for a fourth visit. All High Council rulings and judgements had been put on hold pending further investigation. A steady spell of normality was required before PJ could progress any further in his walk of truth. The breach in balance and time lapse appeared to be restored. Fate, once again was running its true course, unpredictable as ever.

Angus and Anna prepared themselves for an eventual flurry of questions that were sure to come from PJ whenever the shock of events wore off. Anna had already stopped administering her wee top ups of calm, so it was only a matter of time before curiosity took a grip of him. Gradually, he would seek the answers that evaded his memory but left gaps needing to be filled.

In Joe's case, Anna continued giving him small dosages of 'hey man everything's cool,' until she was sure the boy remembered nothing of his own journey, especially the horrific memory of the crash scene on Thorntonhill Rd, which occurred in his true reality and therefore couldn't be removed. These thoughts were buried deep at the back of his mind, behind layers of boring days at work. He wouldn't delve into such things often. The very thought of one of those particularly long, never ending shifts should be enough to make the poor boy lose concentration instantly.

Chapter 15

PJ would undergo changes throughout the next twelve months. He faced a sort of mental obstacle course. These unknown stages could arrive in various forms, leaving him to overcome the hurdle. Each failure causing a steady deviation in direction, every step monitored and catalogued. Sarah and Alex new well the task ahead was potentially perilous but were strictly forbidden to help in any way.

He must prove his worth before being fully accepted by the angelic community. All going well, PJ could graduate with powers at his disposal that would make even the talented young Harry Potter feel like the village idiot. Unfortunately, failure meant taking the wrong path, which led to a doorway, trapping him behind hell's gate for eternity. An added set back was the required participation of the High Council, who were part of a panel of assessors, and also suspended at present. Could PJ depend on unconditional support from a group led by Victor Swift?

Victor was once a brilliant Searcher himself. His kindness and natural instinct earned great respect, leading to an invitation of joining the High Council when the time came for leader, Simon Forbes to move upstairs. Victor was asked to take his place and did so with great enthusiasm and fairness. Then one day, someone noticed a High Council decision not being quite right. Concerns were raised but neither Victor nor his decisions were questioned. Over the next century, more cases arose. Alarm bells starting ringing while silently, situations had to be put right behind Victor's back. Unknown to him, he was now causing a bit of a stir in the angelic world. In his position, an error of judgement could be catastrophic for the poor subject being judged. Someone or something had clearly clouded his decision making. The powers above had to act, sending an important figure to overlook the situation. It was a task, this particular angel embraced with fervour. Simon simply slotted into position as head of the Searchers.

On assessment, Simon found Victor still to be of kind heart and fair in judgement. Something wasn't right, so Simon continued in place as head Searcher. His explanation was that he sought some activity out in the field. Simon would wait on a crack of evidence appearing.

None did, for seventy four years, and then a peculiar case regarding a young family named Timmons surfaced. All were supposed to have tragically died in a somewhat dubious accident. Only one passed away at first, then another.

These were Mr and Mrs Timmons. Before the situation had been properly observed, all four souls were taken. The reverberations however scattered clouds in the right places. A big mistake had, at last come to the surface. In earth time a year had elapsed before the two children joined their parents. Sarah and Alex were orphaned for the final year of their lives before eventually following Mum and Dad in similar strange circumstances. A young member of the High Council was blamed and quickly removed for further training. No harm done, thought some. These were the ones Simon would concentrate on. Sooner or later, true feelings always show. Victor was one of the no harm done, angels.

Over a century later, questions were still being asked. Pieces slowly put together. PJ had added yet another dimension though, both occurrences similar. Simon had almost completed his task. Anytime now, the judgement on matters would be revealed. Meanwhile, Heavens lower levels prayed once again for a peaceful solution. Memories of evil daring to enter Heaven's shores were always dealt with in the severest manner. The older and wiser of the chosen braced themselves. Indeed, this reawakened situation might filter out. It might also lead to another war.

Bridge East kicked off against Thornton once again. It appeared the eventual happening of this game remained an away win. A closer result but never the less, a three –one victory. Jack Watson watched the game with Andy O'Hare. He shook his head in disbelief while trying to explain the recent blurry events. 'I thought I'd hit him?'

Mr O'Hare joined in the headshake alliance, especially reserved for the ridicule of teenage stupidity. 'He's always flying around on that bike.'

Little did he know.

Jack felt just a little too calm and cool for a man who almost killed someone but welcomed the feeling of total relief. He only wished he could stay this way for a few years.

After the final whistle, Jordy Fisher assured his female companion that no further fuss regarding his medical condition would be required. He had already phoned his brother to drive the boys home.

'Wise decision Mr Fisher,' said Aster.

'Can't take a chance driving the guys after my wee turn. Call me Jordy dear.'

'You're a good man Jordy.'

They followed the crowd back to the changing rooms. Aster smiled, but her heart wept. Why couldn't the entire world look at life through the eyes of Mr George Fisher? He was a master of human existence.

The minibus departed for Coalbridge. Malky nodded dutifully as Jordy issued instructions on drop off points. He hated driving the old heap. It only seemed to function properly for Jordy. 'Easy on the clutch man!'

'You're going to gie yourself another bad turn!' ranted Malky, ramming the gear stick into fourth.

Amidst the celebrations inside the minibus, PJ and Joe held important discussions on tonight's dates with Sarah and Julie.

'I bumped into her on Thorntonhill Rd,' commented Joe, as if reassuring himself that he had indeed actually met the beautiful girl.

'I was there mate, remember,' replied PJ.

'PJ stop that blooming bike rattling off my seats son,' yelled Jordy.

PJ smiled down to the front while clamping his bike against the seat. It was great to see the old fellow back to normal. 'Sorry Jordy.'

Loud music thumped down from upstairs at Haystone Rd. Sarah and Alex were getting ready for an evening out at Brannigans.

'I think a small sherry is in order,' said Angus handing the glass to Anna.

'To another success,' she smiled.

'To many more!'

They raised their glasses, momentarily looking up in the direction of pulsating sound, before swallowing. Traces of colour shook free from the vibrating unlit diamond ceiling light, scattering spectacularly in all directions. Their short burst of life enhanced the fading sun, bidding its leave for the evening.

Saturday night also registered as a success. Brannigans offered an escape route that allowed the young Searchers to be normal boys and girls for a while. The world's problems would lie stale and uninvited, expelled to disperse among those who sought trouble on the exterior. Any rude gate-crashers were ushered back out the front door by loud music and laughter. There was no room inside the club for worry tonight.

PJ and Joe made an over the top fuss introducing their female companions. Sarah and Julie pretended not to hear the unconscious compliments afterwards. Sid Savage was overheard asking PJ if the babe thought he was loaded or something. Stevie Dunn stated far too loudly that Joe's girlfriend got around really well for a blind person. 'Well, she must be blind to go out with him.'

Normality gently eased herself somewhat cautiously back into Coalbridge. How long she would be welcome only fate and time knew. For now though, the weekend of repetition took its rightful place in the past. It allowed Monday to arrive without any odd events other than a wage rise from Mr Watson when the boys got into work. PJ could sense a feeling of guilt emulate from Jack as he spoke but simply said 'Thanks boss.'

After an evening spent at Haystone Rd, PJ climbed the stairs to his bedroom, ready for a good night's sleep. Lying in bed, his tired brain signed off instantly. A comforting dream carried him towards the smiling face of Sarah. They walked barefoot over soft golden sand, feeling a slight cooling sensation each time the tide sent frothy blue water across their path. The fresh sea breeze suddenly grew stronger, scattering sand around while blowing into a familiar raging storm that shot them up through the air like a bullet from a gun.

Rushing wind forced PJ's eyes firmly shut, though Sarah's tight grip on his hand reassured him. Still, he couldn't quite rid himself of unpredictability as they hurtled through time and space together.

Sarah's grip suddenly turned ice cold, causing a searing pain to rise up his arm. He quickly opened his eyes. 'Arghhh!'

The creature, a skeletal figure with loose flapping skin, dressed in black robes returned an even more piercing cry as its bony fingers dug into the flesh on his hand. He felt scorching heat momentarily before his body froze in the clutch of his new ice-cold companion. A burning cloud lit up the dark void ahead, blood red in the centre. Yellow streaks of fire splintered in all directions. Helpless to alter course, PJ braced himself as the fiery cloud fast approached. 'Where's Sarah you ugly piece of ...'

He didn't get the chance to finish his question. The creature laughed while they shot into the flame like a diver entering a pool of water.

PJ felt anger build up inside. This new angel experience wasn't going too great so far. His girlfriend had disappeared, leaving him flying through fire with Mr Skeletor. The growing urge to get violent overwhelmed him. He blinked then fully opened his eyes. At least it brought him to an important conclusion. Yes, they were still flying inside flame, but without burning. Fire hissed and curled around them without inflicting any pain. He gripped the creatures black robe, pulling himself towards it.

'Where is she?'

The demon pulled PJ even closer still.

'Worry not. You will be with her soon!'

'Oh well, that's comforting,' said PJ, swinging a glancing punch that landed inside the hood of Mr Bones. 'Arghhh!' He may as well have punched a brick wall. His blow certainly inflicted pain but only to himself. Skeletor seemed to enjoy the moment, releasing horrible laughter to mock the boy's efforts and his obviously really sore right hand.

An underlying desire to hurt the creature took over. Pain turned into inexplicable rage. He struggled to free his other arm, lashing out as they continued their flight inside the glowing furnace. He gripped the creature below the hood, where its neck should be. 'Do you like that, what's the matter, cat got your tongue?'

The demon winced as PJ squeezed tighter and tighter until his hands came together gripping the black garment in a fist. 'Bring her back now!' he shouted.

'Fool, she lies in your conscience as do I!' spat the creature.

PJ released his grip. Mirrors appeared in the empty eye sockets of the demon's skull giving a frightening glance of his startled reflexion. It caused PJ to become breathless. Life began to drain out of his numb body as he tried desperately to free himself. The creature grasped him - close. From inside its hood, Sarah smiled back at him.

PJ wakened, sweating and breathing heavily. This dream had to be up there with the worst of them. It took him several minutes to regain composure before lying back down. Eventually, he drifted off again, this time free from, Bones the demon. Only Sarah's face revisited his sleeping thoughts.

Coalbridge harboured a further three days of non- freaky happenings. In this time, PJ had a few niggling questions answered. He found out that someone, unknown so far, had altered his fate before first contact with Sarah and Alex. In regards to the issue of Mrs Muir and Mr Milne not being in the forest in this reality, Angus explained that a little mind intervention was used to keep the route clear. Mrs Muir and Mr Milne both did venture through the forest on Saturday, but a little later than planned. Angus also advised PJ that he may experience some strange dreams over the next few weeks. 'I think we can use a stronger word than may,' replied PJ, enlightening the group on Monday night's unconscious adventure.

Friday came along in ordinary fashion, handing out helpings of positive mental attitude to the needy. This was in itself, quite a task. PJ and Joe however, required no such pick me ups. They were taking Sarah and Julie to the pictures tonight. In fact, old Mother Nature spent a fair bit of her own day trying to persuade the boys to vacate cloud nine. Early evening breezed in and continued dispersing that Friday feeling among the optimistic dwellers of Coalbridge.

PJ exited the shower thinking mainly about Sarah. After consulting Angus and Anna, she had promised to take him to the 67 cup final at the weekend. He had one leg in his jeans when a text message bleeped from Joe. 'Catch up later, meeting Julie at 7.' PJ sent back 'No probs,' flung the phone down and finished dressing. He momentarily let his mind cast a shadow of doubt over Joe's relationship with the girl he met before the Thornton game but dismissed the worry. Joe was happy for now.

At precisely one minute past seven, the bizarre happening world re-entered his life. It arrived in the form of another text, this time from Sarah.

'Come over ASAP, Joe in trouble!'

PJ tried phoning Joe while sprinting over to Haystone Rd. The number rang out into oblivion as if either Joe or his phone had left the planet. After the events of July 5th anything could be possible. PJ arrived at Sarah's, sweaty and breathing heavy. She greeted his quick response by dragging him inside, slamming the door behind them.

Up on the mid landing, Angus and Anna stood behind Alex. They were concentrating in that familiar, here we go again way, towards a painting on the wall.

'What's going on?' asked PJ, joining them upstairs.

The focus of attention seemed to be a blank canvas set in a dark oak frame.

'It appears Master Watson has been put in harm's way,' answered Angus.

Too busy looking for answers from his friends, PJ was unaware of the colour and shapes emerge through the empty canvas. His eyes widened when he finally turned to the wall. A bustling town scene had sprung to life, set in the form of a bright photographic print. A horse drawn cart looked to be moving lazily along a street full of people dressed in old-fashioned clothes.

PJ wasn't paying much attention to detail or colour. Two particular characters stood out, walking hand in hand. The boy wore a long brown rough textured coat. Pale white legs stuck unwillingly out the bottom of three quarter length trousers. On his head, was a flat cap at least two sizes too big. PJ tried keeping his composure but couldn't stop the nervous burst of laughter that escaped, when recognising Joe and Julie. At least the girl didn't look out of place, dressed in deep pink. Her long gown complimented by a matching bonnet.

'Why are they dressed like that?' said PJ, slowly removing the smile.

'Because somehow or other, he's in 1874,' replied Angus.

Anna stepped forward and placed her finger on the centre of the canvas. It had the effect of a small pebble being dropped into a still pond, causing the picture to ripple in circular little waves that splashed and vanished softly against the thick wooden frame. Once settled, Anna studied the scene which now featured the horse and cart further away. She seemed satisfied with this view. Joe and Julie were trapped in mid motion, crossing the busy road in front of the oncoming cart. Anna touched the canvas again, making more swirling movements. They waited patiently for the picture to become motionless.

The horse and cart had escaped capture in the updated version, having proceeded out of view. Joe and Julie were now at the bottom right of the picture, unaware of the friendly eyes observing their progress from far away.

'There!' exclaimed Angus in a raised voice. He pointed at a crowded area of pavement across the street from Joe and Julie. A brightly coloured sign bordered in diagonal red and white stripes, hung above the doorway of Duncan's

Ironmongers. Directly below, stood a tall, thin, intimidating figure dressed in black, making a hopeless attempt at blending among the people around him. His face carried a sneer as he watched the youngsters pass by. Narrow-eyed cruel intention lay evident in the cold stare from Victor Swift.

'He doesn't seem to take a hint,' offered Alex to an audience of quiet anticipation. Anna sent the picture into rewind. Her angry touch caused the frame to shake as the canvas rippled back through time. It stopped where Joe and Julie were about to cross the street. A shadow from an alleyway rested on the pavement behind them.

Anna pointed to the gap. 'This is where the doorway will bring you out.' Her brief instructions were aimed at Sarah and Alex. Further detail was not necessary. Having carried out many similar tasks, they were fully aware of risk and requirement.

'When do we go?' asked PJ.

His statement certainly brought reaction but not in the manner he had expected. The group turned to him, casting an overpowering glance of pity that spoke more than a thousand words.

'It's too dangerous,' insisted Sarah.

Rigid determination answered their pitiful concern. 'I'm going,' he replied.

'This retrieval could be yet another trap,' said Angus.

'Who cares, I can't just sit back and pretend life is normal when it's not. It might be part of my walk of truth. I'm going,' answered PJ angrily. He noticed the look of shock transmit into something more worrying from Anna's face so decided to finish his outburst in a pleading manner. 'Please!'

It worked. Anna gave him a soft smile and issued some final instructions. 'Stay close to Sarah and Alex at all times.'

'Thanks.'

Anna and Angus moved aside, leaving the three young Searchers standing within touching distance from the picture.

'Good luck,' added Angus as he and Anna quickly headed downstairs.

Sarah and Alex moved to either side of the new recruit. They joined hands and watched the motionless picture. Colour began to bubble and run onto the frame.

'What happens now?' enquired PJ.

'Now, we go bring our friends back. We'll try and have you home for ten,' laughed Alex.

The painting vibrated into life as Alex spoke. Tiny pieces of picture peeled off, rushing past their heads in a frenzy of circular motion, quickly becoming a wall of colour. PJ tried to keep focus but could see only blank canvas through the growing whirlwind. He felt Sarah's grip tighten as the frame rattled noisily on the wall. It exploded, spreading dark shade among the fast moving colours, trapping them in the eye of a great storm that raged around them. PJ momentarily thought of the strange dream encountered on Monday night where he and Sarah were catapulted into a dark void that turned into a blood red sky and a liaison with the skeletal demon that looked like it had escaped from a biology laboratory, after stealing a Monk's robes.

Visions of Victor Swift and his council members swirled around, as did memories of his past adventures since meeting these mysterious angels. Good and bad thoughts flooded in. Apprehension filled PJ's soul as everything became a swirling blur. Was this task a rescue mission or another High Council trap? He would soon be hurtling towards the answer. Sarah turned to him. Her glowing smile breathed new found confidence into his floundering spirit.

'And so it begins, are you ready to do some good in the world?' she whispered.

PJ smiled before the rushing wind forced him to close his eyes.

'Sure, I think.'

Bang. The picture frame rattled slowly, returning the staircase into empty silence. It scratched to an eerie halt, undamaged and still. The young Searchers were gone, off once again, into the unknown.

Chapter 16

Fresh coffee gurgled almost angrily in the pot. Things didn't look too familiar to the old man this morning. Silver framed photographs encased smiling faces and memories that issued him with the feeling that he should remember but couldn't. Perhaps he was just feeling poorly today. He breathed in deeply, enjoying the coffee aroma while filling a 'Greatest Granda in the world' mug. After a slow sip, he trundled over the ceramic tiled floor stopping at a Christmas card view from the kitchen window. Large conifer trees lined both sides of a massive garden, ending at a high red brick wall. Other than the subtle hint of colour from the wall, everything else resembled a white wonderland, glistening under an early morning sun. 'Beautiful.'

He placed his mug carefully into the sink, taking another glance around the family kitchen.

'Where in the name of God am I?'

A hollow metal sound clicking distracted the pensioner causing him to drop the Granda mug. He watched it shatter in different directions on the hard tiled floor, and then began the task of retrieving the broken pieces. He dropped the shattered pieces precariously into the waste bin, releasing the pedal as it disappeared among various rubbish. I can't even remember getting a Granda mug. The bin snapped shut.

Sunlight glared through obscured glass, sending crystal like enhanced colour shimmering its way from the front door throughout the hall, making him blink as he left the kitchen. More silver framed photographs complimented the pale yellow walls, drenched in added warmth from the stained glass door panel. As well as not being able to remember any of the faces staring at him, he couldn't quite recall acquiring such an exquisite front entrance to his home. He shook his head in frustration while heading for the source of sound that caused him to drop the mug. It was a pile of letters, now lying untidily on the welcome doormat. One letter hung clumsily, trapped in the corner of the letterbox. He swiped the thin white envelope free from its metal capturer and focused on the name. It was addressed to a Mr Joseph Watson Snr.

He turned again to the wall photographs, paying more attention to detail but still no memory came forth. A setting sun stooped over a family, holding tall glasses aloft in celebration. Another showed kids on their knees circling a small puppy. An inscription on the bottom of the frame read, Charlie's birthday.

Nope, don't know Charlie.

The next picture was of some old man with what looked to be his wife, standing proud while cradling a new born baby. The old lady looked familiar. It was only then it occurred to him. What do I look like?

He took a few short steps to the wall mirror. Wide eyes greeted his reflexion. Sure enough, he was the old codger holding the baby. Below the mirror, on a glass topped telephone table sat a small metal framed wedding photograph. It was him. He could remember looking like the young man, arm in arm with the beautiful bride. He just couldn't remember his beautiful bride. The old guy carried the photo frame back into the kitchen deciding that whether or not he could remember this young girl, he must be a lucky man. Perhaps when she comes home, everything will fall into place.

Ages away, in another time dimension, a grey mist swirled around the top hall of 11 Haystone Road, where a moment ago the young Searchers had just departed on the journey to retrieve their friends. Anna and Angus waited until it cleared before returning up onto the mid landing where the wall picture swung slowly to a stop. The street scene looked exactly the same, only this time it excluded Joe and Julie. Victor Swift, who had been paying particular attention to them, was also missing from the updated version. So far, so good, the Searchers were half way through their task.

Sarah arrived first. By the time Alex followed, she was already making her way along a bright hallway. A door at the end hung slightly ajar, allowing shadow a brief glimpse inside.
Alex grabbed her arm. Sarah swung around but continued walking.

'How could this happen?' he asked, trying to keep a hold of her. She answered only by shaking her head before pulling the door open, letting in more darkness. It mingled with the light then followed them outside. Alex slammed the door closed behind them. They stood in the narrow alleyway. High sandstone buildings either side offered only a hint of grey sky. Not enough light though, to disperse the gathering shadow, dancing around them.

'Run!' shouted Sarah, giving Alex a helping hand by dragging him by the scruff of his neck. He instantly obliged, overtaking her easily. 'What about PJ and Joe. We're supposed to be going the other way!'

'They're already gone,' she answered while dragging him left, into another alley.

It wouldn't be long now for the impatient creature waiting around the next corner. Demon eyes glazed over, reminiscent of Hell's burning fire. He found a peculiar comfort leaning against the cool stone. These two young Searchers would be easy pickings to such a superior being. Uncomfortable memories always accompanied these short visits. Useless thoughts of skin, touch, feeling, caring. The Demon scorched its discontent deep into the sandstone. Each breath sighed a hatred towards pointless humanity. 'At last.'

The creature moved, hearing the oncoming footsteps. Soon, the annoying children would be in his grasp. Soon, they would be at his master's wish.

Angus and Anna sat in silence, each contemplating different scenarios of tonight's events. It had been five minutes since the young Searchers set off on their journey. If they didn't return in another five, something was definitely wrong. Simon would need to be informed. Only he could summon them back from wherever they were.

Each second ticked away noisily on the grandfather clock over in the corner of the sitting room. Angus was unconsciously combating the frustration by nervously tapping his right foot at every tick, which didn't alleviate Anna's own concerns. 'Must you?'

'Sorry,' replied Angus, instantly stopping the foot movements.

A soft crackling came from within the unlit fireplace. Bright flame danced into life. The grandfather clock suddenly stopped ticking as the burning embers coughed and hissed before spilling out over the hearth onto the Oakwood floor. Angus and Anna jumped to their feet, transfixed on the strange occurrence. The flame grew higher and higher until flickering into a burning rage. A creature appeared, consuming the fire. It heaved and sighed, adjusting to the new environment. Flame burned deep inside the muscled torso, wandering eyes scoped the room then found the gaze of Angus. The demon bowed.

'Angelus, time has allowed us to share another moment.' Its glaring eyes then captured Anna's stare. Her pity unsettled the creature who bowed while regaining composure.

'I am known as Angus now.'

'Your company, gathered along a misguided trail leaves my soul bewildered old friend.' The demon's insult towards his female companion annoyed Angus. He motioned for Anna to sit as he stepped closer to the beast.

'Show no haste Angelus,' it added, shuffling backwards slightly in reply to Angus's advance. He stopped eye to eye, staring carefully through the burning sockets that could easily scourge the very soul of any who allowed themselves to be captivated within.

'Why have you come so far from your beloved master?'

'News of your pathetic new friends,' hissed the demon.

A door behind Anna swung open. Simon entered, wasting no time on greetings he headed straight for the demon. Angus stepped back as it bowed and began retreating into the fireplace. Simon waved a hand, beckoning it to remain still which the creature complied with, waiting head bowed as he approached.

'My fallen brother,' Simon's words carried honest sadness. The demon kept eye contact with the floor while answering.

'Our reminiscence of pathways to glory and misfortune are not shared brother.'

Simon laughed briefly then returned a solemn smile that made the creature look up. Eye contact with Simon was obviously painful going by its hideous body shaking.

'Where are my friends?' The question sent the demon into a spasm

Simon sought the answer quickly in the fury of fire within the creature's eyes then released the beast from further pain. 'Be gone from this World.'

The demon bowed and disintegrated into the fireplace, leaving only a moment of high pitched screaming. Its attempt at offering the Angels a time wasting truce had failed and better still, backfired.

'We must act fast,' said Simon, watching the departure of the creature. 'They have scattered them throughout different time and space dimensions. Simply retrieving them in the normal procedure is not an option due to the added involvement of Master Watson and Julie. Our quickest and easiest method is to remove them immediately from whichever existence they reside at present, before they're moved permanently out of our reach.'

'The after effects can be lasting but under the circumstances I agree, let's bring them all back now,' offered Anna.

Angus nodded his head to the request. Within seconds, the group were out of the sitting room and up the staircase to a room not used for a long time. The bright white walled room contained no furnishings or fittings other than a circular wooden raised area, situated in the centre. It resembled a sort of stage awaiting an entertainment act, which would be coming shortly.

Once all three were on the platform they held hands and looked up. The four walls began moving clockwise, faster and faster, revolving into a circular spinning chamber. When it stopped, the plain white ceiling had become black. Speckles of light appeared, moving dark cloud around dizzily until creating a perfect night sky. Among the shimmering selection of stars on display, five stood out prominent in size and glow. 'Look how far apart they are.' Anna's words were followed by a stark warning from Simon. 'Be prepared, other eyes watch our progress.'

Their merged concentration rose up into the dark sky, stirring the five bright stars like a bowl of soup. The darkness quickly spun itself into a white blur but instead of a golden cloud descending into the chamber, three bolts of lightning shot down, piercing the angels through the chest, pinning them to the floor where they stood.

Simon looked down in disbelief. His hands were already wrapped around the protruding beam that became a cold solid mass on touch. It cooled in a second, turning blood red. Angus and Anna were in the same predicament. The stabbing rods stretched up into oblivion. Horrible features formed around them. Creatures, ghastly in sight, scorned the abrupt silence, wailing hideously. As if trying to fight their way out of a ghostly womb, the demons battered and banged against a transparent shield around the three, trapped angels, but to no avail.

Entry to the chamber was impossible so the obvious reason for the intrusion must be to waste a little more time. Holding the piercing rods in both hands, the three angels lowered their heads in silent prayer. Colour in the rods drained to pale white. The ceiling shuddered violently as once again the cold metal became cracks of lightning, gone in a flash.

Silence returned with the departure of the failed invasion, leaving the angels staring upwards at the simple, night sky. Again, an invisible gentle breath caressed the stars into movement. This time though, small lines broke free from the swirling mass, like glitches to clay on a turning potter's wheel. 'It's no use. They are too far apart. We must bring them back individually!' exclaimed Angus.

So then, began the task of bringing the youngsters back safely, in the order they left. First would be Joe and Julie, then the others. The ceiling spun to a blur for a few seconds, whirring up a thick, golden cloud that slowly descended to the floor. When it cleared, an old man stood, gazing around at his new surroundings. Bewilderment was almost comical in the old fellow's expression. If it hadn't been bad enough spending a morning in a house with no memory of the place, he was then hurled through a black void into another strange abode. He felt some rekindled recollection of the staring, smiling faces. Anna took his hand, leading him from the raised area. 'Joseph?' she asked quietly.

'Anna,' replied the old man.

'Joe, it is you?'

'Dunno.'

The golden cloud was already clearing once again as Anna stepped up to join the others. Julie arrived in a panic. Beautiful and young as ever, she headed straight for the old gentleman who stood in the corner of the room, scratching his head.

'I couldn't get to him,' she pleaded, rushing past everyone.

'He'll be fine dear, don't worry,' replied Anna.

Golden cloud dropped and cleared to reveal a shivering, frightened boy. PJ looked puzzled. An attempt to lure him into an alternative future had failed yet again, but he had felt his conscience starting to battle the evil enticement before being dragged free from its grasp. He said nothing as

Anna put a comforting arm around his shoulder and led him over to Joe and Julie.

'Alright mate,' asked the old man.

'Who are you?' answered PJ, eyeing the old boy up and down, sure that he should know him but couldn't remember his name

'Dunno.'

'Your mate has got himself into an old mess,' said Julie with a relieved smile.

'Joe, look at the state of you!'

The ceiling appeared to be going into overload. Simon seemed concerned as cloud stopped halfway down, hanging still, in mid air before continuing to the floor. It eventually thinned to show Alex and Sarah. Alex looked a bit relieved. Blood trickled down from his nose, dripping off the wide smile he gave Anna. Sarah remained silent, standing behind her young brother, reluctant to let go of the firm grip on his shoulders. Their bodies looked racked with cuts and bruises, some hidden beneath torn clothing. Sarah seemed unaware of the deep scratches on her face.

'She was awesome back there,' said Alex, breaking free from his sister's grasp.

Anna tried to disguise her look of horror. She wiped at the blood, smearing the young angel's face while taking him off the raised area. Angus made a feeble attempt at diffusing the situation.

'I'd hate to see the state of the other guy.' He turned and followed Anna when he noticed her distant stare. Sarah met the welcoming eyes of Simon. 'Welcome back Sarah.'

Slowly her gaze met his. 'They tried to take Alex from me again.' Traces of hatred filtered through, disguised only slightly in her uneasy calmness.

Simon nodded. 'You have performed well child.'

'Why didn't you let me finish it off? They will never leave us alone.'

Simon moved forward, taking hold of her blood soaked hands. 'You did what was required,' he insisted.

'Do we ever?' Her words were cold and uncaring.

'Soon, you will be able to deal with such beasts purely by thought.' He placed his arms around her and held the angry girl close, whispering. 'We ask that in our own time of need, the Lord shall witness the goodness in our souls.'

Sarah slumped into his safe grip and wept the anger away.

'I'm so sorry Simon, I really hurt the demon,' she cried.

Simon flicked her head up to meet his assuring gaze. 'The poor creature was already hurting.'

Sarah accepted the kind words from Simon but knew as he did an important line had been crossed. Far away, unworldly evil celebrated a small victory. The beaten creature crawled back amongst its own, hurt but jubilant.

In protecting her brother, Sarah had not only allowed anger and hatred to take over but actually welcomed it. Traces of these feelings would remain inside her, trying to surface. Evil intention now had a welcoming chance at enticing this hatred out, to suit its own means. Try, these Demons most certainly would. The Searchers needed to be more careful now, than ever before.

Chapter 17

Simon gathered the newly returned group together with Angus and Anna in the sitting room.

'It's good to have you all back safe, though a little worse for wear,' he said.

'You're right there!' muttered old Joe.

'Shut it, you old git,' remarked PJ.

Anna made light of the comment by insisting that PJ show some respect for his elders. Joe backed it up, telling him he wasn't too big for a good slap. It made PJ smile for the first time since being freed from his ordeal, which pleased Anna to see.

'Somebody get a mirror for this old guy,' laughed PJ.

A small debate ensued between the two friends until Simon intervened politely, telling them there would be plenty of time later to carry on with their disagreement. He went on to explain that a recuperation period was now required after such an ordeal. PJ and Joe would need to stay and enjoy the hospitality of Angus for a while.

'We'll have to get home. Our parents will be going off their heads!' demanded old Mr Watson.

'Your parents won't miss you. I must be on my way, Angus will explain,' smiled Simon before bowing to everyone and exiting the sitting room. He probably should have told the boys to rest while they can, but decided against this unnecessary caution.

It took Angus a while to explain to PJ and Joe that although staying with him, they had already returned home and were living pretty normal lives.

'How can we be? Look at me, I'm about eighty years old,' enquired Joe.

PJ looked him up and down with a nod of agreement, and then they turned back to Angus.

'Don't worry. How can I put it? Your soul is here in body while the rest of you is at home,' said Angus, enjoying their bewilderment.

'If this is my soul, you can keep it,' answered Joe.

'You're a young man at home. When you waken tomorrow everything will be normal here too,' explained Angus.

'No more stiff back?'

'I'm sure your back will be fine.'

Everyone laughed, even Joe. Anna and Angus glanced at each other, relieved at the atmosphere and proud of the strong spirit, evident in the youngsters after such a harrowing episode. Evil had once again imposed itself on them. Once again it had failed. In this house though, no harm could befall anyone. They would be invisible to the outside world and the unworldly beings who sought to pursue them. Time could pass, and heal, like only time can achieve.

As the group sat chatting, it became clear to Anna that eyes were beginning to tire. She suggested they leave further conversation until tomorrow. Old Joe was most thankful of the idea. 'My backside is aching, sitting in this chair.' Everyone followed slowly behind the shuffled steps of Joe who was too tired to bother how ridiculous he looked.

PJ had avoided eye contact with Sarah during the earlier conversation, probably due to the shock of seeing her beautiful features scratched and battered. He had also felt her deep upset as she hung to Simon, while weeping her heart out. Not knowing what to say to Sarah, he tried at every opportunity to simply look the other way. She had noticed this also and took his hand as they exited the sitting room. 'I keep getting you into trouble,' she said, making an attempt at humour.

'It sure seems that you're good at getting people back out of trouble.'

Sarah seemed a bit embarrassed by his compliment. She lowered her head as they followed the rest of the group through another door in the hall which took them up a spiral staircase. It came to an end at two large oak doors. Angus held the left door open. Old Joe never broke stride as he entered the new hallway. Julie shook her head and smiled.

'Goodnight Joseph.'

'Yeh, Yeh, whatever.' The old fellow didn't even look back. Alex walked in behind him. Julie followed Anna into the other doorway after everyone bid each other goodnight. PJ found himself alone with Sarah. Angus and Anna smiled and let go of the doors, giving them some privacy. 'You had us worried for a while,' said Sarah.

'I was a bit worried myself for a while. Alex was pretty impressed with his big sister tonight,' replied PJ. 'Alex fought bravely.'

'Do those cuts not hurt?' PJ pointed to the deep scratches on her face.

'Not really. I'm more hurt by showing the demon anger and spite.' Her focus seemed to wander far away, going through the sequence of events with the would-be tormentor, turned victim. Her eyes finally met his. 'We're all back safe now.'

'Will you tell me exactly what happened?' asked PJ, in a truly concerned voice.

'Of course, but not while I look like this. Oh well, time for bed.'

PJ pushed the door open, wedging it against the wall with his back. Sarah leant forward giving him a slow peck on the cheek on her way past. 'See ya.'

She made her way along the hall. At her door, she looked back along towards PJ and smiled at him. He tried to return a cool wink but his nervous cheek muscles gave the impression of sand being thrown into his left eye. Sarah entered her room. He let the door close and made his way into the other hallway. Angus waited along at the third door. The first two doors were closed already. Alex and Joe would be sound asleep by now. 'This one's yours young man.'

'Thanks Angus. I'll sleep tonight, see ya.'

'Goodnight. We're really proud of you.' Angus headed for the fourth door.

It took PJ a few moments after entering before realising he had just walked into an exact replica of his own bedroom back home. The fitted wardrobe full of his clothes, chest of drawers, bedside cabinets, even James' bed was in place. A door led to an ensuite that resembled his family bathroom. Favourite towels, tooth brush, everything appeared to be there. PJ was too tired to question how this could be. By the time the shower switched off, he felt totally refreshed and more importantly, at home. Once back in the bedroom, he sunk down onto his bed, flicking off the bedside lamp. He decided this was probably the most comfortable he had ever felt in his life while drifting off into a deep, dreamless sleep.

Morning slipped silently into afternoon allowing PJ to enjoy time in their company.

PJ wakened with a startle. After a quick yawn and stretch, he contemplated getting out of bed, but not just yet. The neatly made bed opposite only helped to confuse him. It took a few more minutes of relaxed thought to remember last night. James would never be sleeping in this replica bedroom. Enough incentive had been achieved. PJ bounced up, washed, dressed, and decided that company was required. In familiar comfortable clothes taken from the lookalike wardrobe, he made his way along the strange hall and down the spiral staircase. New-found enthusiasm of how his friends would look today rescued him from increasing worry. It felt strange knowing that he was staying with Angus but also living back home. At the bottom of the staircase, laughter and loud chat directed him towards yet another dining room. This house must be massive, thought PJ as he entered amid various cheers of 'Afternoon!' and 'He's up at last!'

'Alright,' replied PJ slotting into a gap between Sarah and Joe. 'You two look a lot better today,' he added while helping himself to a variety of fried goodies nestling in glass trays on the centre of the table. After twenty minutes or so, Anna and Angus rose and began clearing the dishes away allowing the youngsters to sit chatting.

'What did I look like as an old man?' enquired Joe. Julie laughed and replied 'Old.'

'You were about three inches taller than me,' said PJ. Both boys had always been the same height as far back as they could remember.

'Excellent! We're going to be over six feet tall mate,' remarked Joe, pinching a sausage from the dish Anna had lifted. 'Still hungry dear?' 'Just greedy, sorry.'

'Aye, if these creatures stop trying to kill me,' answered PJ, not realising his words drifted around the dining room as a stark reminder of the very reason they were all congregated here today. The remark ended light conversation for the duration of the afternoon. All thoughts turned to last night. Joe rubbed at his imaginary sore back while trying to recall getting a text message from Julie telling him to meet her in Main St. She was adamant that no such message was sent. Meanwhile, Alex explained in detail, his and Sarah's ordeal at the hand of the ferocious demon.

Sarah and PJ sat silent, half listening while reliving their own personal nightmares over and over again hoping some sense or reason could be found. Nothing assuring surfaced.

'Let's all go through to the conservatory. We have a guest awaiting us,' said Angus, doing his best to remove the downward spiralling atmosphere.

Simon was already sitting as they entered. He greeted everyone before giving a complete briefing on the High Council. Victor Swift was still at large but would soon be apprehended. His colleagues couldn't explain the sudden interest in PJ but all things considered were now being very helpful with enquiries. This didn't mean they were innocent of any wrong doings.

Simon instantly put everyone at ease with his update. He finished off by telling the younger members to enjoy their time here with Angus. 'The food is great.'

'It sure is,' agreed Joe.

Angus opened the patio doors. Fresh air began to clear the stuffiness within the glass room. 'It's a beautiful afternoon, why don't you all enjoy the sun for a while?' he said.

'I will need to speak to everybody involved in last night's fiasco, when I return,' added Simon. He bid them farewell and smartly left the conservatory with Anna and Angus.

'Wow! Has anybody actually looked outside?' exclaimed Joe, standing at the open doors. The others followed him out onto a large patio, leading to a sparkling, clear swimming pool. Tension from last night's events faded as they rushed into the house, heading for their rooms. Five minutes later they were all back in the garden dressed only in bathing costumes.

So began a holiday of sorts. Keeping yourself occupied is always easier when there's a pool to splash around in. Everything else required to entertain teenagers lay at hand. Angus seemed to have it all. Tennis courts, crazy golf, swing ball, even the simplistic enjoyment of chucking a Frisbee at each other helped to mend them. A few days were quickly lost in a week, then two, three. Nobody noticed as life drifted past. Homesickness was always going to kick in at point. It happened first to PJ, then Joe, who some days, still didn't know whether he was a teenager or a pensioner. One minute he would be enjoying a computer game before going into a rant about how things were much better when he was young. His tantrums usually ended with him criticizing the youth of today while rubbing an imaginary sore back.

During the few weeks of recuperation Simon had been having frequent chats with the youngsters. He was aware of their desire to return home but couldn't allow it until Victor Swift had been apprehended. Anna took over the task of keeping them busy. She invited the boys to get involved in keeping a watchful eye on the other PJ and Joe who were living normal lives back home. Well, almost normal.

'Let's start our viewing on your return,' she said as they sat, eagerly anticipating a glance at life the way it should be.

'That's my room,' explained PJ as Anna flicked the screen into life. She pressed buttons on the small remote control in her hand.

'Actually, it's your room just before we sent you both back. Earlier in the evening, you had received a message from Sarah explaining that Joe was in trouble.'

'That's right,' agreed PJ.

A tiny clock on the top right of the screen showed a time of Ten Fifteen PM in digital form. The room lay familiar, quiet and empty. Anna fast-forwarded the stillness into blurry movement as she continued. 'You both arrive home to play a bit of X box after simply being out for a few hours.' Anna pressed the play button at Ten Twenty. 'Everything has been monitored since your return'. She placed the remote down. 'Watch what happens.'

Everyone had now gathered in front of the large TV screen. PJ and Joe sat back, fearing the worst. PJ was sure he heard sniggering as Alex, Julie and Sarah joined them on the couch.

Right on cue, the bedroom door swung open. In walked the other PJ and Joe. 'Were on the TV mate,' laughed Joe.

'Is this not an invasion of privacy?' asked a very cautious PJ.

'Any private or personal moments are automatically overlooked and certainly not recorded,' answered Angus.

'Then why am I still very worried?' said PJ, watching the scene unfold.

The boys grimaced as their TV counterparts wandered across PJ's room. TV Joe sunk down onto the bottom of the bed, propping his head against the wall with a pillow. TV-PJ went through the normal procedure on entering his room, power on, television on.

'Fifa?'

'Aye, whatever! Pass me my controller over mate,' said a tired looking TV-Joe.

'Lean forward and get it yourself.'

'I can't, I feel weird,' explained Joe.

'Right then Weirdo, move your lazy bones forward and lift it.'

TV-Joe was already fast asleep. His heavy breathing made TV-PJ feel drowsy. He blinked slowly, trying to rid himself of the unwanted sensation. Each blink though, took him further and further away. His control pad dropped to the floor as he slumped back in the computer chair, into a deep sleep.

A shadow weaved across the floor, caused by the door being reopened. Little Annie strolled mischievously into view. 'PJ waken up, what's wrong with you?' whispered his wee concerned sister.

Meanwhile back in Angus's sitting room tension grew.

'That's sweet. Your young sister is worried about you,' said Sarah, nudging PJ in the ribs. 'No it's not. You don't know her,' replied PJ, sitting forward.

Another shadow traced a path across the TV screen to join Annie. 'They're probably drunk. My big brother snores like that when he's been at the pub,' insisted the other young girl. 'Do you know what I did to him the last time he came home in that state,' she added.

'What?' enquired Annie, eyes open wide with excitement as her friend Rebekah went into detail on the ten minute make-over given to her own brother while in his state of contented bliss. 'When he wakened up and noticed, Mum told him it was what he deserved for getting drunk.'

'Really!'
'Yeh and he got grounded,' smiled Rebekah.
'But there's two of them this time so we'll need help from the other girls,' she advised.

'Let's try wakening them first, just to be sure. Then we'll go get our stuff,' decided Annie. The two small girls proceeded to push and prod at the sleeping teenagers until satisfied that they wouldn't be disturbed while carrying out their creative art.

'What harm can two wee lassies inflict before we waken up,' said Joe, as if he was reassuring himself.

'I hate having to tell you this fact mate but prepare for the worst. Annie was having a sleepover that Friday night with her five pals. She finally moaned my Mum into submission after three long days of, but all the other girls are allowed sleepovers!' replied PJ.

They watched in horror as six little figures appeared on screen. The girls quietly gathered around their victims, while sitting various implements and different sized shiny boxes down. 'Aleigha and Catherine, will you do the boys hair? Me and Natalie are going to do the make up,' whispered Annie.

'Me and Mel will do their nails,' added Rebekah.

'Tell me Annie isn't holding a Tattoo set,' pleaded Joe.

'It is mate, and that other wee lassie has a box of curlers in her hand,' answered PJ.
'Right, that's it. I've had enough. Remote control please,' demanded Joe, heading for Anna. The comments caused a tidal wave of laughter as she handed the small box over to him. He pressed the fast forward button, whirring the screen into quick motion for thirty seconds. It stopped abruptly, returning to play as the sleeping boys were getting Hannah Montana tattoos stuck onto their foreheads. Joe pressed stop. The screen went blank.

'That's a shame. I wanted to see your hair when the curlers came out,' laughed Alex.

'Tough luck then ain't it,' smirked Joe, trying his hardest not to burst into laughter himself.

'I think we've seen enough,' stated Anna, wiping the tears from her eyes.

'I'm glad you all found that wee show amusing,' said PJ, doing his best not to smile.

'Sorry boys, we couldn't resist it. Besides, I thought the young ladies did a great job with the lipstick,' joked Angus, causing more sniggers.

'Could I have a private word with the boys please?' asked Anna, through a warm as usual smile. The sitting room cleared instantly leaving her alone with PJ and Joe. She pressed the rewind button until the screen once again returned to an empty room. A digital display panel flashed across the bottom. The information read July 11th, 1 of 38.

'Surely that doesn't mean there's another 37 horrendous things still to happen?' enquired Joe.

'No, it means day one of thirty-eight,' said Anna.

'We've been here for thirty-eight days. What date is it back home? PJ suddenly became interested, as did Joe.

'August 17th,' she answered.

The boys' minds went into overdrive wondering what they had missed. The summer football league would be finished. Did Bridge East win? Big decisions were supposed to be made regarding staying on at school. 'Our exam results will be in,' said Joe, beginning to look rather worried.

Anna went on to explain that their counterparts back home were perfectly capable of dealing with any arising issues. She asked the boys to follow her out into the hall, across to another room. It consisted of only a comfy looking two seater sofa in front of a similar sized TV to the one in the sitting room. Anna lifted the remote control, pressed a button that brought up the previously viewed bedroom where the boys make over was just about to commence once again. 'You can use this room to catch up on home events,' she said, handing the control to

Joe. Julie arrived into the room. 'Mind if I join you?'

'Sure, but I'm not watching those wee lassies attacking us again,' replied Joe, taking a seat.

'Spoilsport,' she said, bumping down next to him.

PJ returned to the sitting room. Sarah was already waiting. 'Let's see how you got on with your exams?'

'I want to make sure we won the league first!'

This task kept them busy for a few hours. Bridge East had indeed won the league. Both boys passed all their exams and were currently at home preparing to go back to school in the morning. A lot of the viewing was dull though, without any sense of fun. It appeared that the other PJ and Joe plodded through life in an efficient procedure like manner, much to the delight of their parents. In short, they had become boring. The highlight of the evening remained Annie's make over.

PJ's thumb was beginning to get sore from continually pressing buttons when Anna burst into the sitting room. 'Come quickly! Simon has arrived with important news!' she exclaimed while grabbing PJ by the arm and dragging him in the direction of the dining room. In front of them in the hall, were Joe and Julie, being pulled along by a very excited Angus. 'Are we going home now?' asked PJ.

'Let's wait and see what news he has for us. All going well, you could be sleeping in your own bed tonight,' replied Anna.

'Greetings,' smiled Simon as they entered.

Chapter 18

Victor Swift looked to be physically worn done as he sat alone in a small plain room of cold grey stone. The bland surroundings had gone unnoticed while interrogating subjects in this very place through the ages but that was all in the past for him now. Harsh reality stung his heart and watery eyes. Victor awaited a decision that would shape his own future and destiny. When did he begin losing interest in such things? A young, innocent soul had almost been lost because of Victor's arrogance and stupidity. Paul Joseph O'Hare nearly paid the price for a son begging to be reunited with a lost cause of a father. Victor felt ashamed for his actions.

After talking at length with Victor, Simon had held an even longer discussion among colleagues in the next room. This meeting came to close only minutes ago. Victor swallowed uncomfortably as he heard the angels head off up and down the corridor. Each click of their heels brought added dread to his sickened soul. He knew though, whatever the judgement may be, it mattered little to him now. Too much damage had already been done to his character. Once trust has been lost, is it ever really found again? Trust indeed, was the main agenda of the meeting. Disappointment of course had constantly arisen throughout the talks, but it was mostly due to honest concern for an old friend. Everyone agreed that Victor had not acted quite like himself for almost a century. Cases for and against the accused were brought up in abundance.

How could he have missed that one? Remember the entire Village he saved! The debate rumbled on until finally arriving at the main agenda, Luthor Swift. This man lived a life of hardship, much the same as many before and after him. He grew up harbouring great thoughts and dreams that faded slowly with the passing years. By the time Luthor married Edith and became a father to Victor, his path to villainy shone bright as shooting stars lighting up a night sky. Earn an honest living had long since turned to take what you need to provide a great living. How easy it had become to rob thy neighbour as opposed to uselessly loving them. 'What charity were we ever given freely?' Luther always reassured himself with these words when returning home from each trip.

Edith welcomed him with open arms. She was so proud of her hard working husband. He would always have a special gift for young Victor, who was allowed to sit up late on the evenings of his father's arrival home from work. She never knew exactly which business her man involved himself with. It seemed to change, as do the seasons. Edith rectified uncertainty by explaining to her rich new friends that Luthor bought and sold things. Somewhere inside, she hid fear of anything more sinister, while ignoring occasional remarks. How can a travelling salesman afford such grandeur?

Victor benefited from a good, wealthy upbringing. Strict rules from both parents kept him well mannered while Luther's ill-gotten gains educated the boy. As a result, Victor Swift had a great deal to offer a confused, aggressive world. He set out to change it. Unfortunately a twist of fate truly tested the strength of the young man. One week before his eighteenth birthday, news arrived of the untimely death of Luthor. Any explanation of the accident lacked in detail. Edith may have been told more but gave no further account to grieving son Victor.

Eleven months after the sad passing of his father, Victor had to grieve again. Edith tried her best to carry on but found life without her childhood sweetheart just too much to bear. The poor lady unconsciously died from a broken heart. This dragged the high-spirited young man down into the pits of despair. How could God have taken his parents who were only in their early forties? How could God have left him alone in the world? All of Luthor's so called family friends had long since departed. Victor suddenly became a lonely, bitter person.

On the day of his mother's funeral, an unusual man introduced himself as an old acquaintance of Luthor. He sparkled with character and charisma. Victor instantly befriended the cheery, thirty-something fellow, who helped restore his faith in humanity and put him back onto the path of life, which ultimately lead to Victor being known as Father Swift. During a long lifetime in the priesthood he would meet his soul's saviour only once more but never forgot the importance of their two- month friendship or the lessons taught by Nathanial Flyte.

'A flame of strength burns brightly in your heart. Take care holding the fire. Should it ever burn out I will return holding a candle,' smiled Nathaniel to the eager young Victor before they parted company. The kind words weren't only a reassurance of friendship but a promise. It instilled even more ambition to achieve goals without any personal gain.

Victor went about life. Too busy helping others to notice the flame start to flicker. Friends who gathered around the old priest saw him simply smile at an empty space at the foot of his bed before taking leave of life. No one saw the return of an old friend keeping a promise.

Only Victor witnessed the truth and the prize offered by Nathaniel. A chance to continue in his life's work was the gift given to a soul not ready to rest. The new angel welcomed his new task with open arms. Victor now held the simplistic knowledge of humanity. He took further comfort knowing his mother waited at the end of his quest. He also had to hide the disgust and disappointment of finally finding out his father's worth. The man who taught him right from wrong was nothing more than a common thief, lying in limbo. His tally of sins was the amount of years he would spend in this suspended state. Easy research advised Victor not to expect a chat with Dad for a very long time. On the very day of receiving this news, a seed of hurt rooted itself deep into the good intention of a being that thrives on making things right. Throughout the next two hundred years the seed blossomed slowly into a wild flower of hope. Victor allowed its presence only momentarily at intervals when his concern didn't involve the wellbeing of others.

On one of these rare occasions he had a visit from Nathaniel telling him there was a possibility of an early reunion with his wayward father. Victor knew how much this would mean to Edith. Surely she deserved peace and fulfilment after living such an honest life?

'No one will suffer who doesn't deserve to,' promised Nathaniel.

Victor's eyes momentarily lit up with excitement before narrowing into a suspicious glare. 'What must be done?'

Nathaniel who led an efficient team of angels overlooking discrepancies had found a flaw in the system, one which could be used to allow entry from limbo before a soul's correct time. They needed only to monitor the situation to make sure no mistakes were made while searching for Luthor. Nathaniel explained there would be another soul to be sought out, his own father. This was the added incentive behind Nathaniel's plan to help a friend. Both angels sealed an unwritten pact on that very evening.

Victor wiped regretful tears away from under his eyes as he thought back to the stupid selfish idea created by two sons longing to reunite their families. The extent of damage was not yet fully calculated. Although he felt almost sure that no souls had been lost during their century of searching, Victor made himself another promise. He hoped and prayed for enough time to make amends. His father would need to wait for now.

The door to the small chamber opened sending fluorescent light across the cold stone. Amelia Longthrift entered and bowed. Victor shuddered with embarrassment as the angel spoke. 'I am so sorry to hear of your plight.' She quickly moved aside. In walked a cheery faced chap in his mid thirties. Victor stood instantly and returned the angel's gesture of greeting with a quick bow. He could not find a smile for his oldest of friends. 'What have we done?'

'Nothing that can't be undone,' answered Nathaniel in a meaningful reassuring voice.

Amelia bowed again and closed the door, leaving the angels to a much needed chat.

Simon waited until all were seated before proceeding with his latest update. A cheer went up from the younger listeners on the news of Victor being apprehended. The celebrations weren't shared by Anna and Angus. 'I knew he was up to something,' stated Anna.

'What exactly was he up to?' added Angus

Simon went on to explain the real reason behind Victor's strange behaviour. By the time he told the sad tale of a man wishing only to witness his mother and father in lasting peace, Victor Swift had unknowingly and most probably against his will, received undivided support and overwhelming pity from the group.

'What will become of him now?' asked Sarah, concerned and deeply upset at her own lack of judgement. Before Simon could answer the question, Joe piped up with his own uncertainties. 'He set a trap for me and Julie.'

Simon smiled while shedding light on that particular incident. Victor had become aware of another attempt at interfering with PJ's destiny by using Joe as bait. He had to follow up the matter at once, without time to inform anyone of the plan. Before Victor set off after Julie and Joe he asked a trusted colleague to pass on the message. 'That important message arrived too late to be of any use,' stated Simon.

'Who is this so called friend?' demanded Angus.

'I'm afraid it was none other than Nathaniel Flyte.'

'I don't understand it. Why would he do such a thing?' said Anna, disbelief etched across her face.

Once again, Simon filled the group in regarding Nathaniel's own dilemma. Similar circumstances had forged a strong bond between two hard working unselfish angels. 'We must accept part of the blame for never finding out how Victor and Nathaniel really felt.'

'They should have trusted someone enough to speak about their true feelings,' replied Anna.

'Easier said than done. I think we're all guilty sometimes of harbouring mistrust, pride and arrogance. Never the less, these are the charges they must answer for,' explained Simon.

A short silence followed, while everyone absorbed this latest spiral of events. Eventually, PJ spoke. 'Does this mean we can go home now?'

'Not at the moment but very soon. Although Victor and Nathaniel monitored the breech closely while searching for their fathers, we must find the creator of the flaw in the system. Hundreds of angels are reviewing each case, tracing it to a source. Their work is almost complete. When it is so, we will have a name. Only then can we truly…

A door facing PJ opened, in walked Aster giving a wicked smile to all before bowing.

'Greetings,' she said.

'Please sit with us,' insisted Angus, already on his feet pulling out a spare chair next to him and Anna. 'What news do you have?' he added.

Aster thanked Angus for his kindness, sat, flicked her hair into accurate beauty over both shoulders before continuing. She set her gorgeous gaze towards Simon. 'Your colleagues have completed their task.'

Simon acknowledged the comment but looked as if he could have done without hearing the outcome. He simply nodded his acceptance for the answer.

'All roads lead to the same unwinding path. Nathaniel Flyte seems to be at each journey's end,' stated Aster.

Simon nodded but didn't appear too surprised. It was as if he presumed Nathaniel had more to answer for than simply meddling with a flaw in the system. He addressed the youngsters. 'Could I have a private word with Angus and Anna please?'

'Yeh sure,' replied Sarah, leading the way out of the dining room. They took their seats in the sitting room. Alex and Sarah began a deep conversation about the unfolding events so Joe and PJ chatted themselves. 'So how is your other self - doing?' remarked Joe.

'I've turned into a boring git.

'Me too,' laughed Joe. 'We need to get back home and save ourselves before we turn into geeks', he added.

'Aye! Before Annie has another sleepover. Anyway, have you stopped feeling like an old man?'

'More or less but I still get a bit stiff now and again,' said Joe rubbing his imaginary sore back. He leant forward towards PJ, with a serious look on his face. 'All joking aside mate, what's going on here?'

'I'm not really sure to be honest,' answered PJ, wondering when Joe last had a top up of calm from Anna.

'Do you not think this is all just a bit strange? We've just been watching ourselves on TV because we've got doubles!' exclaimed Joe, his raised voice beginning to carry fear.

Sarah arrived beside him. She placed a hand on his forehead then returned casually to her seat. Joe stared at the floor for a few seconds before resuming conversation. 'More or less but I still get a bit stiff now and again.' He rubbed his back, unaware of repeating himself.

PJ smiled once more while drifting into thoughts and concerns of his own. He could hear Joe babble on in the background but wasn't really listening to the restored, happy-go-lucky guy. Stark reality was paying a visit. This is all my fault. Joe needs constant calming to stop him flipping out because of me. The poor guy got stuck in an oil painting, almost fell victim to a hideous demon, and even thinks he's a pensioner sometimes. He's witnessed so much, then had memory of such things erased like simply deleting a programme. Another harrowing thought gate crashed uninvited. Soon, they would be returning home. Soon, Joe would be, once again oblivious to the madness of PJ's new world, as instructed by Angus and Anna who insist that Joe must have no recollection of events. Soon PJ would find himself alone.

A warm rush of comforting peace suddenly seeped through, obliterating any uncertainty, no matter what lay ahead. He slowly gazed up to see Sarah remove her hand from his forehead.

'Are you alright mate?' asked Joe, bewildered by the strange behaviour.

'Aye, I was in dreamland there.' PJ watched Sarah retake her seat. She smiled at him before getting back into conversation with Alex. Another instalment of, everything is going to be fine, had been successfully administered. Sarah waited until the boys were discussing if there was a possibility of avoiding the humiliating make over by Annie and her pals before taking another peek. PJ seemed to find her wandering eyes. He knew hardship would never be faced alone. A voice echoed around his head in a soothing manner. Ensuring words slowly drowned panic and dragged it back down into the caverns of forgetfulness, where it would dwell among horrible memories such as Bert Travis and his tracksuit.

These top ups of calmness were beginning to be required more frequently. At first, the boys needed only one touch from Anna to see them through an entire day. The necessity grew steadily over the month. Yesterday, PJ had to be given four, while poor Joe received a total of nine. If matters weren't concluded soon, someone would have to follow Joe around the house holding his forehead. For now though, both boys were comfortable and calm.

'Could everyone come back through to the dining room please?' said Angus, startling the youngsters with his sudden appearance at the open doorway.

An unsettling atmosphere awaited them. Anna and Aster were in deep conversation, speaking too low to be heard but stopped and smiled almost nervously as they all sat. Simon remained on his feet. PJ and Joe got the distinct impression of being the reason of tension.

Simon smiled at the boys before talking. 'You will be able to return home tomorrow evening. Use this last night to decide on which date would be preferred for arrival back to normality.'

'Can we go back to the first day of the summer holidays?' asked Joe. His face wore an expression of already knowing the answer but thought it was worth a try.

'Choose only from when you arrived here to stay with Angus. Good choice though!' added Simon.

'It's got to be Friday 11th.' exclaimed PJ. 'Another month off school and a chance to miss out on getting attacked by Annie and her pals.'

'I agree,' Joe nodded his head in firm support of PJ's decision.

'So it shall be. You will both be unaware of the luring text message, while preparing to spend an evening with Sarah and Julie. This should ensure not missing out on going to the pictures and also a chance of avoiding the wrath of six little girls.'

The boys looked at each other in a most serious manner before reinforcing the decision by nodding in unison. Simon acknowledged their wishes with a courteous bow. 'I need to speak with everyone individually please, before I leave this evening,' he added.

'Of course,' stated Angus. 'You and Aster can use the sitting room. Who do you wish to speak with first?'

'Young master Watson. It's only a quick chat Joe. Don't look so worried.' Simon's reassurance helped slightly, but couldn't totally wipe out the boy's reluctance of trusting anyone while such bizarre thoughts and recollections raced around his head like a roller coaster. They entered the sitting room.

Simon wanted to make sure Joe had fully recovered from his pensioner ordeal. Once the three were sitting comfortably, he let Aster captivate the boy in conversation allowing him to reach beyond the bravado. Her smiling face was enough to lower his well-guarded shield. Simon had been keeping close tabs on Joe's progress and hoped for better findings. It wasn't to be. He searched through protective layers of humour, still finding inner feelings that shouldn't visit a young man in such a way. Confusion brewed among dismay and discontent. Each new dosage of calm received, would work for no more than a few hours before having an adverse effect. Joe was already experiencing weird, interrupted dreams where his friend had been knocked down and killed. Visions of the driver being his Dad haunted increasingly more of his sleeping hours. Unfortunately, this mind calming now interfered with previously hidden memories. Joe was beginning to recall things that he shouldn't. Simon listened in to the conversation.

'Where did you meet Julie?' asked Aster.

Joe lowered his head while trying to remember. Eventually he raised his head. 'I met her the day we beat Thornton. She was there when PJ nearly got hit by my Dad's car before the game.'

Simon and Aster didn't even get the chance to breathe a sigh of relief before Joe added

'I'm sure I've seen her in a painting.'

Enough had been said. Joe needed to be freed from these increasing living nightmares once again.

'This time tomorrow night, you'll be back home with your family,' promised Simon. They chatted about the make over from Annie and her pals, winning the league and passing exams. Simon erased the uncertainty and upset as they spoke but made a mental note to ensure that the boy returned home with the unwanted memories buried deeper this time.

Chapter 19

'You're next mate,' exclaimed Joe, swaggering into the dining room. He bumped down onto the sofa, snuggling into Julie. PJ got up reluctantly and headed for the door. Before leaving the room, he turned back to Joe. 'What's with the stupid grin?'

'Dunno? Probably because we're going home tomorrow,' answered Joe, already paying full attention to Julie.

PJ walked slowly towards the sitting room. He felt relaxed but tired. Simon stood and motioned for the boy to sit opposite him and Aster.

'Joe appears excited at the prospect of going home to normality,' smiled the beautiful female angel.

'Yeh,' replied PJ, not even bothering to conceal the envy that accompanied his answer.

'I think his brain is a bit fried,' he added.

'The more a brain is relaxed the more open minded a being becomes. Joe has almost reached the point where concealed memories will no longer be hidden. He shall travel home tonight,' explained Simon.

'Does he know?' asked PJ, looking a bit baffled and feeling a bit bewildered.

'No, he is probably planning how to spend his last day before going home. The next time you see your friend, he will remember nothing of his stay here.' Simon paused before adding, 'we would like you to stay another day. Joe will have his slate wiped clean again.'

'Your slate however, still presents us with difficulties,' added Aster.

'Don't I know it,' agreed PJ.

Simon reassured the worried boy. 'Spend some time with us tomorrow. Joe's future, your future, our very own, are but blank leafs of paper on which we bear witness and record eventual decisions. Why you have been chosen to work as one of us remains unclear at this stage. One clear fact has emerged from our latest findings though. You now have a choice. If, by tomorrow evening you wish not to accept this proposal then I promise that nothing will interfere with your future destiny.'

'Both you, and Joe will simply forget all about us,' smiled Aster.

'What if the council enforcers come back to my house?' said PJ, wondering at the possibility of returning home to a normal life.

'Normality means the normality you were used to, before first contact with Sarah and Alex. The world of angels and demons will not exist in your lifetime,' explained Simon.

'What about the walk of truth. I thought you said it had already begun?'

'Your journey will be put on hold. Life's experiences and choices carve out their own path. Sooner or later, every soul attempts the walk of truth, either in life or death,' added Simon.

'If I go home then I won't get all these super powers Alex told me about?'

Simon and Aster laughed at the boy's refusal to let matters get on top of him. Aster answered,

'You won't need super powers, or us. She paused momentarily before adding, 'Or Sarah and Alex.' The bombshell had been dropped successfully.

'Do not make your decision in haste. We shall discuss the matter further tomorrow,' advised Simon.

PJ nodded his understanding of the advice given. It seemed a luring temptation to turn his back on this disturbing world of good versus evil. He could go back to being PJ O'Hare, the day dreaming boy, living a simple life. No one in their right mind would rather get up in the morning and check the calendar to find a circled reminder, (1pm meeting with demons from hell)

He looked up to see Simon and Aster already standing, waiting for him to withdraw from his trance of thought. 'Erh, sorry! See you tomorrow then.'

'Goodnight,' they replied, watching him venture back into the possibility of 'what if?' as he departed the sitting room.

PJ stopped in the hall. His eyes caught a fleeting glimmer of light cascading from a photo frame sitting on top of an old teak writing bureau just outside the dining room. He approached the family style snap sure he hadn't seen this picture of Angus and Anna before. The old couple stood side by side. In front of them, smiling attentively was Sarah and Alex. PJ stared at the photograph. These four angels had well and truly got under his skin.

The door to the dining room lay open. Everyone must have retired for the evening. He went in and sat at the end of the large table. PJ could have done with some company right now. The earlier words spoken by Simon raced around his head. Normality means normality. Sooner or later every being must take the walk of truth. Life's choices carve out their own path.

Angus entered and sat next to him. The old fellow took a sip of brandy then twirled the crystal glass around in his hand. 'It appears that you have a get out clause young man.'

'Yeh,' answered PJ watching Angus take another slow drink. He placed the empty glass down and yawned. 'Oh well, time for bed.'

'What should I do?' asked PJ.

Angus casually rose to his feet. 'I think you should wait and see what tomorrow has to offer before worrying anymore.' The elderly angel lifted his glass then bid the confused boy goodnight.

Alone once more, PJ added this new advice to his dimension of thought. More of Simon's words filtered through. The next time you see your friend, he will remember nothing of his stay here.

If the future was indeed just blank leafs of paper waiting to bear witness and record eventual decisions then how could Simon be so sure that I won't pop into Joe's bedroom on the way to my own. If he's sleeping I could waken him up. What if he freaks out again like earlier?

PJ instantly decided to follow Simon's advice, though he felt deep down that it was actually an instruction. Either way, he knew it would be for the best.

'Not tired dear?' Anna stood in the doorway. Her soft spoken words released him from delving further. He jumped to his feet. 'Erh, hi Anna, I thought you were all sleeping.'

'Angus asked me to share a nightcap in the sitting room before retiring. Everyone else is fast asleep.' She could sense distress in the boy's tone but waited for him to answer.

'I was going to check up on my other self before going to bed but if you and Angus are still sitting in there I'll not bother.'

'I'm sure your other self is fine. Get some sleep, we've got a busy day tomorrow.'

'I don't want to forget all of this,' stated PJ before adding 'Goodnight.'

Anna stood at the bottom of the staircase watching the troubled boy as he disappeared around the top landing. She felt sorry for him but knew the answer lay in a muddled heap somewhere in his confused mind. Anna also knew that the boy who arrived into their lives had now, somewhat reluctantly, turned into an adult. He just wasn't aware of the sad fact yet and would most definitely fight against the unwanted necessity until his last boyhood breath.

PJ made his way along the hall, and climbed the spiral staircase. At the top, he stopped at the two doors, tempted to open the one on the right, wander down the girl's hallway and chap Sarah up for a chat, but decided against it. What if she told him to go back home and forget her? Suddenly, the thought of rejection scattered unimportant issues such as his own safety and security, like a cat amongst the pigeons. He realised that a certain conversation with Miss Timmons was essential to his final decision. A surge of relief dropped into his mind in a rushing waterfall that cleared away complication and worry. It left a simple solution to the problem. Sarah would have the last word. She would be the answer he sought. If he was asked to go, then he would do so without hesitation.

PJ pushed the left door open and proceeded past Joe's bedroom to his own. An uncomfortable swish of envy entered his mind once again. Wouldn't it be great not to have a choice? No need for such drastic life changing decisions. A sixteen year old boy should be fretting over worrying issues like where the money will come from to buy the latest computer game or which clothes to wear on a night out. These were the only pressing concerns awaiting Joe on his return to normal life. It seemed a welcome invitation right now for PJ as he slumped down onto his bed trying hard not to work himself up into a frenzy of confusion.

He flicked the bedside lamp off, allowing his galloping mind to return to a slow trot. The dark silence offered happy memories as a substitute for growing anguish. A glowing vision of Sarah filled his senses. PJ drifted into a contented sleep while browsing among recollections of the last few weeks.

Time began to roll forward too quickly then jumped back as each sleeping breath highlighted an unanswered question. The uncertainty spread like an untreated cut, infecting the goodness around it until all that remained was doubt. His dream carried uncontrolled thought, far into the realm of unconsciousness where uncertainty and doubt raced along a path that led to anger. An unfamiliar voice spoke to him. Disguised in soft tones, it advised PJ not to trust his new angel friends. 'They are asking too much of a young man,' whispered the invader of his dreams. 'Go home to the safety of your family before it's too late.'

PJ could only agree but found himself questioning the strange presence. 'Who are you?'

'I am a true friend.'

'Why are you turning me against them?'

'They mean you harm.'

The words echoed with accusation before drifting into cold silence, leaving frustration as a companion to the festering rage.

PJ wakened, breathing heavily. He needed a few seconds to escape the blinding anger. When the sensation had passed, it left behind more confusion. He lay, staring at the dark ceiling while trying to work out what had made him become so angry in the first place but could find no reason for such emotions. 'They mean you harm,' drifted back into his thought as he slumbered back to sleep.

Monday morning gently eased her bright sunshine into the quiet bedroom, inviting PJ to embark on his final day. He was slow to accept. Anna entered and moved a few things around noisily in a further bid to waken him. 'Good morning sleepy head.' No answer.

She approached the bed. A world of worry seemed to have set deep into the sleeping boy's features. Anna placed a hand on his forehead. PJ's eyes slowly opened. 'Morning. Is that my first top up of the day over with?'

'I've given you an extra dose this morning, seeing as it's your last day. Breakfast is ready,' replied Anna. She smiled before making her exit, leaving PJ to shower and dress. By the time he strolled down towards the dining room, body and mind were totally refreshed. Even the concept of knowing his best mate would now, most probably be sitting in a classroom, free from complication, couldn't dampen his spirits. 'Morning.'

'Morning,' replied Sarah and Angus, looking up from their half eaten fry ups.

'You nearly missed the blooming morning,' added Alex, while dipping half a link sausage into the yoke of his fried egg.

PJ sat at the table. 'Funny guy.'

'Did you sleep well?' asked Anna, placing a full Scottish breakfast down in front of him.

'I had a weird dream,' stated PJ casually as he lifted his knife and fork.

'What happened in it?' enquired Angus.

'A friendly voice told me that you lot were bad news.'

The clicking of cutlery on crockery ceased immediately. His statement brought curiosity and silence to the group. They looked at each other; wearing 'here we go again' expressions.

'Did you recognise the voice?' asked Sarah.

'Nope.'

Everyone watched on as PJ got tucked into his breakfast. 'I'm going to miss this black pudding.'

When everyone had finished eating, they cleared the dishes from the table. Angus invited his guests to join him in the conservatory. On the wall, Julie's picture smiled as the group departed the dining room. PJ felt a twang of sadness seeing the beautiful girl trapped once more inside the painting of Inglefoot Fayre.

'It's only a picture. Julie is at home with her family,' said Angus, noticing his concern.

'Why was she missing from the picture?'

'Because she was staying here,' added Alex.

PJ didn't bother asking any more questions about Julie or wall paintings. In his mind though, he craved answers to far greater issues. Hopefully, some light could be shed soon. He followed the others into the conservatory and sunk down onto the couch next to Sarah.

Not wanting to begin his questioning at the deep end, PJ opted for a light hearted opening.

'Joe travelled back home last night,' he stated.

'Yes, without any complications,' answered Angus.

PJ took a moment of thought before speaking.

'Did he arrive back before Annie's attack on us?'

'Yes,' added Anna.

'Well, that's a positive start. At least we got out of our ten minute makeover.'

'Not exactly,' smirked Alex.

'What do you mean, not exactly?'

'Unfortunately you both fell asleep again.'

'Joe is currently in fourth period,' explained Angus, in an attempt at changing the subject. It didn't work.

'So, we got whacked again?'

'I'm afraid so,' admitted Anna.

'Let me try to get my head around this. Joe left last night but by now he'll have been home for weeks living a normal life. Surely he must have noticed a difference in his best mate?'

'Only that you seem to have grown up and are a bit more responsible,' said Sarah.

'In other words, he and all the rest of the clan will be discussing how much of a geek I've turned into. They all must be having a right good laugh.'

'Your mates just think you've got a bit boring, that's all.'

Alex's comment annoyed PJ, especially the way the young angel smiled afterwards.

'Searcher. That's a good word to describe you Alex. You always seem to be on the lookout for a good hard slap.'

'Whatever.'

'No, it's more a case of whenever.'

Sarah intervened, firstly with an angry glare in the direction of her brother, then a tap on PJ's leg.

'He's only messing around as usual.'

'He's an annoying wee git.'

'Sorry,' stated Alex, in a reluctant manner.

'No probs wee man. Try and keep your face on call though, cause you're well overdue a slap.'

'Sarah and Alex are going to take you on a reach and touch exercise today PJ,' explained Anna. Her pleasant tone carried a friendly warning that all bickering should end now. The group complied.

'It's time for you to see how we spend our days young man,' motioned Angus, while offering Anna a helping hand from her seat.

'Let's hope Simon can ease our tension by delivering some good news later,' added Anna.

'We seem to spend most of our wakened hours waiting on news from Simon!' said PJ. Frustration was evident in his raised tone.

Before leaving the conservatory, Anna turned to the youngsters.

'I have a feeling that today will bring us closer to a successful conclusion. Dinner will be at six. Until then...' They smiled then strolled out the room.

Angus and Anna departed the conservatory, leaving the group to work out their own uncomfortable situation. Sarah took charge.

'Ok, let's meet in the dining room in thirty minutes.'

PJ nodded his head in agreement while Alex apologised once again.

'I'm only trying to act like ordinary boys of this time. Everybody seems to insult everybody and nobody seems to take offence. Whenever I try to be ordinary, I always seem to upset somebody.'

'There is a way to do it without actually annoying people too much,' replied PJ.

'But what's the point in that?'

'Maybe you should just try and act like an ordinary boy from your own time. Anyway, I'll catch up with you both in half an hour. There is something I need to check up on.'

PJ exited the conservatory quickly, after his words of advice to Alex. Sarah and the now glum looking boy sat a while longer in the sun drenched glass area, while going through today's missions.

Right, how does this thing work? PJ sunk down onto the sofa, having flicked the switch on. A sky blue glow from the TV lit up the shaded sitting room. He pressed the rewind button until arriving at his chosen date. July 11th flashed along the bottom of the screen. PJ touched stop, paused for a few seconds then pressed play.

Let's see if things have changed now the real Joe is back home. After all, Anna had promised that their counterparts were perfectly capable of dealing with any arising issues. The problem niggling away at PJ worsened as he began viewing. Within five minutes it was beyond a shadow of doubt. Again, Joe had noticed a change in his friend's behaviour. PJ felt a tinge of reoccurring cycle slowly creep in. This saga seemed to be never ending. He hit the fast forward button, again, again. The further on he went, the more embarrassing situations arose. This was worse than first time round. Instead of getting grief from his mates for missing a football game and the odd one or two thinking he actually had gone insane, people were reacting differently towards him. Different even from when fate had supposedly been mended and for a while, everything appeared normal. What would happen when PJ finally returned home, again?

No matter which way the situation filtered out, each time differed from the next. None was better than the other.

The current PJ living back home risked losing his friends for no reason other than he was becoming a bore. Would the freshly enlightened PJ return to a hearty welcome or be alienated as being a smug git. Going by recent events, PJ prepared for the worst. He pressed stop, threw down the remote control and left the sitting room.

Balance, fate, contortion and time lapse.

PJ knew one thing for sure. Life would never be the same unless he asked his new Angel friends to finally wipe his own slate clean, like Joe's.

He was also learning a little more about fate and balance along the way.

Chapter 20

'Alright pal, come in. I see you managed to get that wee wave out your hair!'

'It's not funny. I spent over an hour getting nail varnish and tattoos off,' said Joe in reply to Mr O'Hare's dig at last night's unfortunate makeover. 'I hope she's grounded for a month,' added Joe.

'I only grounded her for a fortnight. They did do a good job with those face paints though. PJ's upstairs.' Mr O'Hare nodded in the direction of the staircase as he spoke.

'Don't tell me he's slept in again.'

'No, he's finishing off tidying his room.'

Joe came to an abrupt halt half way up the stairs. 'You've usually got to threaten him with violence to get him to tidy that room. James always ends up doing it.'

'Yep.'

'What's the matter with him?'

'Who cares, long may it continue!' laughed Mr O'Hare.

'Hi Joe.'

'Don't you even talk to me hen. I hear you're grounded.'

'Aye, but it was worth it.' Annie smiled that victorious smile and closed her bedroom door as Joe reached the top of the staircase. She didn't catch the very short recognition of respect come from the boy who only last night peeled a Hannah Montana tattoo off his forehead. Memories of that bizarre awakening had annoyed Joe in bed last night but not for the obvious reasons. Anyone's initial reaction to wakening up in such a state would be pretty much the same. Joe however, felt deep down that after the shock and fright, surely there should have been laughter. PJ had simply shook his head and shouted on his parents. Now he was tidying his room. Something's not right.

'Alright mate, did you get that Bratz glitter off?' said Joe, pushing the door to PJ's room open.

'Eventually!' PJ continued to fold up clothes and place them neatly in his freshly polished chest of drawers.

'You've got to give them a bit of credit for their idea though. When did you learn to fold clothes like that?'

'I can't believe we fell asleep and let they wee lassies set about us,' PJ answered, ignoring the remark about clothes folding.

Mr O'Hare passed the boys on the staircase. 'So where are you two off to? Let me guess. It's the park for football?'

'Correct Mr O. What about you, let me guess. Saturday morning, that means you must be about to wash the car?' replied Joe.

'I hope you're not trying to suggest that I'm an old bore?'

'Never!'

'Beat it, the pair of ye!'

Joe made his usual useless banter as the boys headed for the park. His partner in crime though seemed to be more interested in discussing other matters. To Joe's horror, even school came up in conversation.

'Look mate, I don't want to sound too ignorant but can we drop all the gumph about the future and options and responsibilities and anything else that involves thinking. Remember our promise on the last day of school. Football and fun! Deal with the other stuff later.'

'I'm only saying that this is an important time for us. The choices we make this year are massive. We need to make the right ones.'

'We're making all the important decisions we need to at the minute. First, a game of football followed by whatever decision we make in a couple of hours' time. You need to chill out a wee bit mate.'

'You need to start acting your age.'

'Wait a second here till I get this dummy tit out my mouth. Right! The deal was, pass our exams, and stay on at school, sorted. So what's the problem? We're doing that!'

'Chill!'

'I was chilled until you turned into your dad!'

'That's a very grown up comment.'

The boys continued their journey to the park in silence. PJ shook his head occasionally as if in a state of disgust. It only fuelled the fire of discontent within Joe, almost to the extent of not really liking this guy any more.

'Alright guys! Ten a side, we'll change at half time,' said Sid. He almost missed the tension between the boys, but noticed something was definitely wrong just before kick off. Joe's shake of the head and serious glare towards his best mate made all around uncomfortable.

'Is everything alright mate?' whispered Sid, as PJ met Joe's look of distain with a 'you need to grow up' stare.

The game burst into life, with shouts of 'Here! Mine! Foul!' but Sid clearly heard PJ answer his question. 'He's always going to be a loser.'

Angus and Anna were already sitting in the dining room when the youngsters arrived. PJ looked miles away as he wandered behind Sarah and Alex.

'Something wrong dear?' asked Anna.

'Everything's wrong!'

'He thinks he's a boring git back home,' added Alex. The comment didn't help.

'I don't think I can do this.'

'You haven't seen what can be achieved. Or the feeling when you've just helped someone change their life for the better,' pleaded Angus.

'But what if you're changing something that shouldn't have been changed in the first place?'

PJ walked over to the window and stared out at the vast garden. Sarah approached and stood alongside him. 'You've got a choice remember.'

'Yeh, I think that's the problem. Why me? Why have I been chosen or picked out or whatever else it is? Simon told me that if I want to forget all of this then nothing will interfere with my future destiny.'

'That's true.'

'No, that's the problem. He only said normality means normality. Simon doesn't know what's happening. Let's face it, my normality hasn't really been normal for a wee while now. Nobody predicted Walter Swift turning bad or why he came across me?'

'I came across you.' Sarah edged her hand into his as she continued. 'Alex and I never had a choice. We just arrived at the mercy of David, who realised something wasn't quite right.'

'That's my next problem!'

'What, David?'

'No, you!'

'Why?' she asked, turning towards him.

'Because, at the end of the day, you were born a couple of centuries ago, which makes you a bit older than me.'

'In my true existence, you are seven months older!'

'Which brings me to my next problem. You're young, you're absolutely beautiful, but you're also dead!'

Sarah burst into laughter. 'You have actually witnessed all of this yet still question life and death.'

'What's funny?'

'Who said I was dead?'

'Oh right, I take it you and Alex just look young for your age!'

Sarah didn't seem to see the funny side of things any more 'We had the same choice as you but our parents were already dead so we wanted to stay with them.'

'That was in 1857.'

'Time is of no importance under these circumstances. Our case has simply been put on hold until a final decision is reached.'

'So, you and Alex could live again as normal people?'

'If we wanted to.' Sarah's smile returned. 'But who would want to live a normal life after being offered such a wonderful gift!'

'But would you get zapped back to 1857 or could you pick a time?'

'PJ, you ask too many questions. Try not to worry about needless things and concentrate on today's tasks.'

Sarah returned to the dining table, leaving PJ staring out of the window. This latest instalment of info churned around inside his brain. Once it had settled, he felt a little more open minded to eventual decisions and less panicky about when to make them.

The group were all seated and watching him as he slowly turned away from the window. Anna sensed a slight tilt of relief from the boy, which would at least help while preparing to get a brief glimpse at a prospective career.

'Take a seat dear while we run through a few details,' she said.

'No probs.'

Anna and Angus went into detail regarding today's agenda. The group would be travelling together to a chosen destination where PJ could try out some R and T exercises. He could remember Reach and Touch very well, seeing as it was this very procedure that brought him into contact with the Angelic community in the first place. They advised PJ that a little help would be administered to allow him to carry out such a task. He thought it really amusing how calmly Anna finished off by stating, 'Then we'll come back for lunch,' as if the group were simply heading out for a walk around a quiet pond.

Angus added that, after lunch, PJ would set off on his own mission, accompanied only by Sarah and Alex, who were there as back up. 'You'll get a chance to use your new R and T skills and hopefully change someone's life for the better.'

PJ's face lit up with sheer excitement that dulled slightly on hearing that he was going to be responsible for another life.

'Shall we?' Anna stood at an open doorway. The group entered a small hall. PJ didn't even moan about the bright white walls as she closed the door. Travelling through doors or pictures or whatever other method were the last thing on his mind right now.

A door emerged on the far wall. 'Where are we going?' asked PJ.

'Shopping,' answered Anna, holding the new door open. PJ followed on behind feeling slightly hesitant.

'So, what now?' He glanced around the enormous retail park. You could buy anything in this place. Carpet and underlay were half price till Tuesday, buy a bike and get fifty pounds off the second one. Some shops were almost giving clothes away. It was a shopper's dream come true. You could even regain any lost calories, brought on while walking around, by visiting one of the many cheap fast food outlets or for a few pounds more, go all out on a three course meal. Any further enticement of purchase would be put to rest on the final shop through Asda.

'Let's mingle for a while,' instructed Anna.

'You can hardly move through this crowd,' replied PJ,

Anna placed a hand on his forehead. 'Relax and look around.'

PJ spent the next fifteen minutes giggling as he passed people. One girl in her early twenties gave him a rude 'what are you looking at glare', another seemed embarrassed by his eye contact. An old man threatened to knock his block off if he didn't stop staring at him with that stupid smug grin.

'Try to control your emotions,' suggested Angus.

'Yeh,' agreed Alex. 'Try and do it quick before somebody hits you.'

'I can't help it. People think a load of mince, don't they!' laughed PJ, while making an attempt at straightening his face. He was being overthrown by constant waves of conversation. I shouldn't have used my credit card. I wish I had got the twelve pack when they're down to a pound… etc, etc, etc.

'If you notice though, most of the people around us are actually thinking about shopping!' said Anna, seeing PJ go wide eyed at some of the ruder comments.

'There is a skill to be learned in shutting out people's more personal thoughts just before they think of them,' she added.

'I did some training in a restaurant once and nearly collapsed because of all the lovey dovey chat around me. These people were supposed to be blooming eating!' said Alex.

'It was after 9pm on a Friday night' offered Angus in defence of the love struck merry makers.

'They were supposed to be blooming eating!' repeated Alex, much to PJ's amusement.

'You are a bit young for all that nonsense wee man!' he quirked.

The group strolled along, almost to the edge of the giant shopping centre. This area seemed a bit less busy. Anna suggested that they sit for a while. From two benches, back to back, they were able to let PJ concentrate on passing shoppers. It seemed the longer he connected with a person, the more uncomfortable the situation became. After brushing through initial thought he was feeling their deep emotions, hope, desire, fear of the past, present and future. Uncertainty and insecurity lay evident in every passer - by. Most of the worry he was encountering resembled his own personal dilemma.

'See the old lady wearing the green hat?' asked Anna.

'With the matching handbag, what about her?' replied PJ. He began latching on to her thought. Her mind was mumbling to him rather than speaking.

'She's forgotten to buy something or lost something, no wait a minute, she's forgotten something!' he decided.

'Well done, now reach further!' exclaimed Angus.

'It's at home!'

'Further!'

'She's left a letter with a cheque in it, on the mantlepiece at home. It's a birthday card for her nephew. If she doesn't post it today, it will arrive late.'

The moment PJ finished speaking, the old lady stopped, looked down as if in deep thought, then raised her head and smiled a victorious smile before turning around. She walked off smartly while shaking her head.

'She's remembered!' said PJ.

'You reminded her.'

PJ appeared a bit baffled by Anna's comment. All he did was listen in on the old woman's ramblings.

'See it as helping her to weed out the unimportant issues to allow more important matters to filter through.'

'So, I actually went into her mind and found what she was looking for?'

'You sure did,' said Alex.

'Cool!'

They spent almost an hour sitting while PJ, successfully helped another old biddie find her husband. Reminded a woman to phone her man to tell him to take the chicken fillets out the freezer and stopped a wee day dreaming guy from wandering in front of a car while searching for a number in his phone. His greatest achievement of the morning though, was reuniting a frantic mum with her lost child. This was the one that mattered most. It left PJ feeling a real sense of purpose and achievement. He would have happily spent the rest of his day wandering around altering people's minds.

'Let's return to Angus's house for lunch. We'll discuss your mission,' suggested Anna, taking PJ by the arm. This morning's R and T exercise had been a success. It was time for the boy to take on the role of a Searcher, at least for a day.

They headed along to the door with the Private sign above. Back in the dining room, PJ rambled on about his new talent. 'Did you see the look on that woman's face when she found her wee boy?'

'What you were feeling was her sense of relief,' smiled Angus.

'Whatever it was, it felt brilliant!' replied PJ.

After lunch Anna sat a brown folder in front of PJ. Inside, lay a brief on his next mission. He flipped the plastic cover over and began reading. The client was a sixty-year old man who had only recently lost his wife. It took fifteen minutes of browsing before PJ closed the folder then turned to Anna. 'This case seems easy enough to solve.'

'Is that so?' she asked.

'Yeh, the poor old guy has been so heartbroken about losing his wife that he's forgotten other people around him. This situation is going to get worse if he keeps feeling sorry for himself.'

'Why?'

'Because he's not speaking to his son.'

'And?'

'His son is so worried about him that he's neglecting his own son.'

'And?'

'The bad feeling is going to go on for over a year. By that time, the grandchild will already have chosen another path in life. My mission is to convince Granda that his family need him more than ever right now.'

'Well, off you go then!' said Anna. She got up and headed over to a door at the end of the dining room. Holding it open she nodded to Sarah and Alex. 'Let's see how our new recruit gets on?'

'Don't let him out of your sight!' warned Angus, just before the door closed behind the youngsters.

Only an hour had gone by when the same door opened. In walked a rather chuffed looking PJ. Anna and Angus sat at the table as the young group took their seats.

'I knew it was the grandson that needed help!' exclaimed PJ before anyone else got a chance to speak. 'They're going to be ok now aren't they?' He looked towards Anna for verification.

'Yes, you've correctly assessed the situation. Mr Collins has now realised how upset his son is. More importantly, as you pointed out to him, life must go on. I think the way you achieved it though, was either luck or a touch of genius. Telling somebody who has just lost a loved one to get over it and get on with it, could have had an adverse effect, but worked superbly.'

'Mrs Collins used to say that to him quite a lot. It's on page four of the file,' replied PJ.

'Using an old familiar line while actually showing the effect of neglect towards his Grandson was brilliant mate!' stated Alex.

'I still don't know how I managed that bit yet?' laughed PJ.

'You identified a perfect example of memory from Mr Collin's grandson, where he needed important advice from his Dad who wasn't there for him because he was worrying so much about his own Dad!' explained Anna.

'Ok, I think.'

'You then allowed Mr Collins to visit this particular memory, where he could witness the extent of disruption,' added Angus.

'But how?'

'A simple matter of thought transfer!' said Sarah, hoping that PJ would lose the screwed up, confused looking face soon.

Alex completed the explanation. 'You put young Peter's thoughts into his Grandfather's memory, which instantly changed the old guy's outlook on life.'

'Hopefully forever!' said PJ. 'By the way, we say Granda in this neck of the woods.'

'Whatever.'

'Can I have another go just to make sure the first one wasn't a fluke?'

'Why not, here's some information on the person.' Anna handed PJ a single sheet of paper containing only a few paragraphs. He read the vague file.

'I think I might need some help with this one!'

'Have a think about it on the way.' Angus held a door open as the youngsters made their way into another familiar bright hallway.

'Greetings!' Simon and Aster gave a quick bow on entering the dining room. Once seated, Simon couldn't disguise his discontent inside a shallow smile. Angus tried to hide his own concerns of the latest news he would soon hear from these serious looking guests.

'Anyone for a sherry?'

'A large brandy please!' replied Simon. Aster and Anna asked for the same as Simon began on his latest findings. 'We traced PJ's memory of the Demon encounter back to Nathaniel Flyte. It appears that the simple flaw in the system allowed other flaws to go unnoticed.'

'Each time Victor and Nathaniel breached the system, a doorway from Hell opened. A split second was enough time to let hundreds of fallen souls enter Purgatory!' added Aster, before Simon continued.

'The Demons lay in Limbo awaiting their chance to progress closer to Humanity. Some made it through. A few worked among the

Council enforcers while others carried out their master's wishes in other areas.'

'Would one of these areas be Witchwood Forest by any chance?' asked Angus, already now sure of the answer.

'It seems PJ is of some interest or importance to their beloved master!' exclaimed Aster.

Simon went on to explain how a strong feeling of wrong doing lurked around Coalbridge on July 5th, particularly within the forest. Sarah and Alex would be of no concern as the Demon hunted its prey. When PJ came along on his bike, Sarah also sensed something and felt compelled to remove him from present time. Only when she was sure that the unknown threat had passed, was PJ allowed to continue his journey. Sarah luckily moved the three of them out of harm's way. The Demon was unable to follow her path in time and had to admit defeat at the hands of two Angel children.

Unfortunately, the poor creature would come across these two young Angels later, in an alley and find out that their strengths far outweighed its own.

'David has an army of enforcers swarming Purgatory at this very moment. Thousands of souls are being discovered hiding among those spirits who are almost healed. His task shall take a while yet!'

Anna sipped the last of her brandy. She and Angus were relieved to hear the news of things being restored but hoped for better information regarding the involvement of PJ. Both knew the sensible solution now was to return him without memory back to normality. Should anything dare approach the boy on his next visit to July 5th then the Searchers would pounce instantly.

'He doesn't need to know all the details right now,' advised Anna. Angus nodded his head in agreement while lifting her empty glass for refill.

'It's the only way to finally free the boy from their grasp.' He added.

'Depending on how tightly they wish to hold on to him?' remarked Aster before casually swigging the remaining contents of her own glass.

Simon handed Angus an empty glass. 'Thanks,' he said. 'I needed that. Allow PJ the luxury of making a decision as planned. It will help us guide his future, if required.'

Angus refilled everyone's glasses as a few moments of silence was shattered by the sudden return of the youngsters, laughing and joking about their latest mission. They regained a bit of composure when noticing Simon and Aster, who gave a quick bow.

The group made their way into the sitting room where Simon began the conversation by asking PJ about his first missions. The boy took great delight in explaining how he helped the Collins family but seemed a bit reluctant to admit he couldn't work out the second case for nearly an hour before realising no assistance was required. This situation had remedied itself on its own, so at least he'd learned the important lesson of unpredictability. Even when people in need pray for help, sometimes things have a way of working out for the best before help arrives.

PJ nodded to Simon's advice then listened as the Angels discussed the events surrounding the flaw in the system. He waited patiently, hoping that the topic would soon shed some light on his own situation.

Eventually, Simon asked him if he had made his mind up yet. The question took PJ by surprise at first but he gathered his thoughts quickly and replied 'Yeh, I'd love to be a Searcher!'

'Then, so it shall be,' answered Simon.

'Have you found out why I got picked out?'

'Not yet, it could be that when the Demons invaded humanity, you were simply in the wrong place at the wrong time. I give you my word though, the next time we meet, I promise to have an answer to your question.'

'That seems fair enough. So, it's ok for me to be a Searcher?'

'Going by your first few attempts I think you'll be a great Searcher.'

'Thanks!'

PJ was just about to burst into a full frontal assault of questioning when Aster reminded Simon of his meeting with the High Council. They excused themselves and departed, leaving Angus and Anna with the task of retiring their latest recruitment, at least for a while anyway.

There was no point in telling PJ the plan, then spend the rest of the night justifying it. So, he would remain under the impression of going home as a new Searcher. The evening consisted of a few more missions before supper. Angus and Anna concealed the truth well but Sarah could sense something out of place, though her senses also recommended to go with the flow.

They finally headed off to bed after a long eventful day. PJ was becoming accustomed to the usual swish of ever flowing thought that invaded his head after such occasions. As far as he knew, his chosen date was Friday 11th which would give him another opportunity to avoid the dreaded make over, and also help remove the geek that impersonated him at present. No harm to the guy but he wasn't doing his reputation any favours. It would also be great to get back to the family again. He missed them more than he liked to admit.

As such contemplations raced around, PJ found it harder to achieve the simple task of falling asleep to allow his return to reality. He lay smiling at today's missions but also had spontaneous visits from more forgettable memories. The journey to Angus's home while under attack from an army of Demons couldn't remove the smiling face of the grateful Mr Collins. It soon disappeared among webs of Council enforcers and attempts on his life.

Football was the answer. PJ focussed on Bridge East. His smile slowly returned as he remembered the look on big Bert Wallace's face each time Thornton lost. It would be great to see the smug git as Bridge East picked up the trophy for the summer league.

'Pass!'

PJ lay fast asleep.

He stared into the scowling face of Coalbridge Rovers captain Stuart Gray. Off he went on his glorious run, after swiftly spinning around the giant defender.

'Pass!'

'No chance! I'm going all the way.' PJ sped past McPherson.

'Pass!'

'I can do this!'

BANG.

PJ gazed up at the cotton wool staircase, unaware of any previous encounter with the weird cloud formation. Tam McAdam came into view. 'Sorry wee man, I hit ye a bit too hard there!'

'Nah, I've been hit harder by the cold.'

'I told you to pass the ball son!' ranted Coalbridge Rovers boss Bob Kennedy, pushing McAdam aside. The spray that accompanied the manager's tidal wave of abuse caused PJ to close his eyes tight.

'Are you deaf as well as stupid!' ranted Mr Kennedy.

'Beat it!'

'Don't talk to me like that! Get up, you're late for work!'

This was the signal, the trigger that sent PJ's confused brain into a fast spin.

'Get up, PJ! I'm not going to tell you again!'

A rollercoaster of muddled thought collected memories and shot them like a bullet from a gun, deep into the forgetful section of his mind. Mission accomplished.

PJ sprung up, his wide-eyed stare caused James to jump backwards.

'Are you alright wee man?'

PJ didn't answer. He glared around the room as if looking for an invisible threat then his wandering eyes sought only an answer, which also fizzled out when making eye contact with his big brother.

'PJ, you're starting to annoy me now pal?'

'Wow! That was weird!'

'What was weird?'

'That dream!'

'What were you dreaming about?'

PJ continued the far away glare towards James. 'Dunno!'

'Whatever, look, get your backside out of bed. I'm off to the sports centre. I'll try my hardest not to mention to Mum about you having a nervous breakdown, but I'm not promising anything. You're definitely getting worse.'

'Cheers.' PJ jumped out of bed, ignoring any further comments from James while heading for the shower.

Twenty minutes later, tie straightened, hair sorted, he smiled at his reflexion in the hall mirror. 'Dreams! Jeezo!'

The end

Printed in Great Britain
by Amazon